# ONCE UPON A KISS

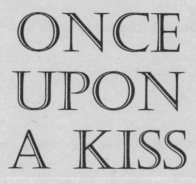

## CAROLA DUNN
## KARLA HOCKER
## JUDITH A. LANSDOWNE

Zebra Books
Kensington Publishing Corp.
http://www.zebrabooks.com

ZEBRA BOOKS are published by

Kensington Publishing Corp.
850 Third Avenue
New York, NY 10022

First Printing: May, 1999
10 9 8 7 6 5 4 3 2 1

Printed in the United States of America

# "THERE IS A CODICIL, ADDED ONLY LAST MONTH, THAT MAY SHED SOME LIGHT ON THE QUESTION OF LADY EMILY'S MOTHER AND BROTHERS."

When the solicitor finished reading, a thick silence hung in the air. The will made no mention of Emily's mother. The codicil, however, did pertain to her brothers. Her father had, indeed, received a report of their deaths in France, but he had strong reason to believe the report was false. He wanted his daughter to find the truth. And to that purpose, she must go to Ravenhill.

Impossible.

"I cannot go!" Emily had come close to shouting at the elderly man and rose hastily to walk off the agitation that threatened to suffocate her.

The solicitor watched her with a searching, puzzled look. "Do you not wish to find the truth, Lady Emily? If your brothers are alive, surely they have a right to their inheritance."

"They're dead," said Cousin Harold. "And I shall start proceedings immediately to have them legally declared dead and buried."

"Which is precisely why Father asked *me* to look into the matter." Emily all but tore the hem of her gown as she strode up and down the study.

"Why then do you hesitate to fulfill your father's wish, Lady Emily?" asked Mr. Wordsworth. She cast him an anguished look.

"Because," Cousin Harold said smoothly, "our dear Emily compromised herself at Ravenhill."

—from "The Seven Ravens" by Karla Hocker

# BOOK YOUR PLACE ON OUR WEBSITE
## AND MAKE THE
## READING CONNECTION!

We've created a customized website just for our very special readers, where you can get the inside scoop on everything that's going on with Zebra, Pinnacle and Kensington books.

When you come online, you'll have the exciting opportunity to:

- View covers of upcoming books
- Read sample chapters
- Learn about our future publishing schedule (listed by publication month *and author*)
- Find out when your favorite authors will be visiting a city near you
- Search for and order backlist books from our online catalog
- Check out author bios and background information
- Send e-mail to your favorite authors
- Meet the Kensington staff online
- Join us in weekly chats with authors, readers and other guests
- Get writing guidelines
- AND MUCH MORE!

**Visit our website at**
**http://www.zebrabooks.com**

# CONTENTS

# ALADDIN'S LAMP

by
Carola Dunn

# PROLOGUE

Though Alan's mind still followed a strand of the tangle of English jurisprudence in the books he left behind, his feet bore him out of the college and round the corner into Holywell Street. As he passed the dusty window of a curiosity shop, a blue glitter caught his eye. A sunbeam had fought its way through the murky glass to sparkle on a string of beads. It reminded him that today was his mother's birthday, a fact liable to get lost in a head full of legal complexities. The necklace would be a good present.

A bell tinkled as he pushed open the door and went in. "How much are you asking for those beads in the window?" he asked the stooped old man who appeared from a back room.

"The blue ones? Half a guinea."

"I'll give you half a crown."

"Ten bob, and that's rock bottom. They're genuine Strass glass, they are."

Even for "genuine imitations," ten shillings was much more than Alan could justify spending on anything so frivolous. He shook his head, but he went on to poke amongst the extraordinary collection of oddments on the shelves.

They varied from a forget-me-not decorated chamber pot with a broken handle to an exquisite ivory horse from China; from odd forks and spoons of both silver and Sheffield-ware to a ship's compass. Alan found a gold watch with a repeater mechanism. He listened to its chime, and was regretfully replacing it on the shelf when he saw the perfect gift.

The small vessel was the exact shape of Aladdin's lamp in the illustration in his mother's favourite book. Pointed at one end, it was rounded at the other, with a curving handle and a circular foot. It would amuse her, and it only needed a wick and oil to be useful, too.

Taking it from the dim depths of the shop over to the counter at the front, Alan saw that his find was heavily coated with verdigris. Cleaning it was going to be quite a chore.

"How much?" he asked.

"A crown."

"Five bob? But it's green with age!"

"Proves it's copper or brass, not just tin."

"There may be nothing left once the corrosion is cleaned off."

With a grunt, the dealer prodded the lamp. "Tell you what, I've had it lying around for years. Half a crown."

"A shilling."

"A florin."

"Eighteen pence," said Alan hopefully.

"One and nine," the man countered.

"All right, if you'll wrap it for me."

Grudgingly the old man nodded. He produced brown paper and string, while Alan dug the coins from his thin purse.

The parcel safe in his coat pocket, Alan continued along Holywell Street and across the grounds of Magdalen College to the footpath on the bank of the Cherwell.

# ONE

"A perfect day, and amazingly warm for May," Lady Beatrice said gaily, as the boat slid out from the willows' shade into a patch of sunshine. Conscious of the admiring gaze of a shabby young man tramping along the riverbank path, she adjusted her pink and white parasol to frame the golden curls beneath her Leghorn hat. "A punt is a delightful mode of transport, is it not, Miss Dirdle?"

Her companion and ex-governess nervously surveyed the smooth, grey-green surface of the River Cherwell. "Delightful," she murmured in a tone utterly lacking in conviction.

"I shan't upset you, ma'am, never fear!" cried Cousin Tom, the young gentleman wielding the punt pole. "Punting's safe as houses."

"It's my turn, Tom," insisted Lord Wendover. Tom's best friend and a fellow student at Magdalen College, he was madly enamoured of Bea, and always trying to impress her. Impeccably dressed in fawn trousers and a blue morning coat, he had tied his starched white cravat so high it held his chin up at an uncomfortable angle.

Tom, in buckskins, a shooting jacket, and a red Belcher kerchief, said scornfully, "Don't be a sapskull, Windy, you can't punt in that rig-out."

Resorting to nursery language, Lord Wendover snapped, "Can too!" as he stood up and reached for the pole.

A brief tussle rocked the boat, till Miss Dirdle's cry of alarm made Tom let go. A moment later, Lord Wendover was left clinging to his trophy as the punt moved on without him. Tom made a grab for his friend, the punt tilted, and Bea found herself floundering in the chilly Cherwell.

Annoyed, but not particularly alarmed, for Tom had taught her to swim years ago, Bea quickly found her feet in three feet of water. She looked around, recovering her breath. The punt, tenantless, was heading downstream for the Isis. Lord Wendover still clutched his pole as it slowly tilted riverward. Tom stood waist-deep laughing at him, heedless of the plight of his cousin and her companion.

"Miss Dirdle!" Where was she?

"I have her, ma'am." The shabby fellow from the footpath emerged from the river like Neptune from the waves, the elderly gentlewoman coughing and spluttering in his arms. "Just let me carry her to the bank, and I'll come back to give you a hand."

"Thank you, sir!" Bea exclaimed gratefully. She started to wade towards the bank, her thin muslin skirts dragging at her legs. Miss Dirdle's heavy bombazine gown ("Ne'er cast a clout till May be out" was one of her favourite maxims) together with panic, must have pulled her down. She might have drowned, but for her gallant rescuer.

He laid her on the grass and turned to help Bea.

"Don't come in again," she said, looking up at the

hatless figure, water streaming from his short, dark hair. "Though you can scarcely get any wetter, I admit." Reaching the bank, she held out her hands.

Grasping them, the young man hauled her out. She stumbled against him and he caught her in his arms, but he let her go at once. As he stepped back, one hand out to steady her, their eyes met.

For an instant, an electrical current seemed to sizzle between them. Bea lost her breath again.

Then his gaze rose to her hat and he said, a quiver in his voice, "I fear your bonnet will not recover from its ducking."

"N-no matter." Her voice quivered, too. "I shall enjoy shopping for another. I must thank you, sir, for saving my companion."

"It was nothing." His eyes dropped and a slow flush rose in his cheeks. Hurriedly he turned away, stripping off his sodden coat. "I hope the lady . . . Ma'am, are you all right?"

Miss Dirdle sat up, gasping. Dye from her black bonnet streaked down her cheeks, and the bombazine adhered to her bony chest. Bea took a step forward to join the old lady.

The young man stopped her and thrust his coat into her hands. "Here," he muttered with apparent confusion, "it's no drier than your . . . than you are, but . . . but . . ."

"Lady Beatrice!" cried Lord Wendover, sploshing up onto the bank. "I say, I'm most awfully sorry."

"Bea, you *are* a sight!" That was Tom, of course.

Bea looked down at herself and realized that her gown clung like a second skin. With renewed gratitude, she shrugged into the stranger's coat. He was tall, so the tails reached almost to her ankles and concealed—from the back, at least—the greater part of her exposed figure.

He was leaving, at a rapid stride. Bea hurried after him, as close to running as allowed by her wet skirts and Miss Dirdle's rigorous training in ladylike conduct. She caught his shirtsleeve.

"Sir, how shall I return your coat?"

Half-turning towards her, but not looking, he mumbled, "Alan Dinsmuir, at Wadham College, ma'am."

The patched cambric slipped from between her fingers, and he hastened on.

"Bee-ya!" Tom called.

She paused for a moment, staring after the young man, hugging his coat about her. Had she imagined that shock of awareness between them? It had struck her like the jolt from the electrical apparatus Tom once brought home to Hinksey Hall. Mr. Dinsmuir must have felt it! Or had his voice shaken because he was trying not to laugh at her disgraceful appearance?

Alan's feet bore him automatically across Magdalen Bridge, up Headington Hill, and through the village. He was unaware of the stares as he passed soaking wet, hatless, in his shirtsleeves. Before him floated a piquant face with golden curls, and rosy lips parted in a saucy smile, and eyes the blue of a cloudless summer sky—which yet had the power to strike a man with lightning.

His gaze still on this vision, he came to his mother's cottage, a short way beyond the village. Opening the gate in the high hawthorn hedge, where bees hummed amidst the may-blossom, he crossed the tiny garden in a few strides, and stepped into the low-ceilinged, stone-floored kitchen-parlour.

Mrs. Dinsmuir dropped her sewing in her lap. "Dearest," she exclaimed, "what *has* happened?"

"I have just met the most beautiful girl in the world, Mother," he answered dreamily.

"And she robbed you of your best coat and hat, and pushed you in the river?" Mrs. Dinsmuir asked in horror as he stooped to kiss her.

Alan returned to earth, glancing down at his sodden clothes with a rueful smile. "No, she was boating on the Cherwell with a couple of oafs who overturned the punt."

"So you pulled her out?"

"Not even that, alas." He sighed. "She found her own feet and was obviously safe, whereas her elderly companion went under and failed to reappear. I had to find the old lady first, so I cannot even figure as Lady Beatrice's gallant rescuer. Yet she thanked me as prettily as if I were. She is the dearest creature!"

"*Lady* Beatrice," said his mother, dismayed, "the daughter of an earl, or marquis, or even a duke. Alan, pray do not set your heart on a female so far above your touch."

"I'm hardly in a position to support a wife of any sort, Mother, far less one accustomed to a life of luxury. I cannot even support you." He scowled at the needlework she had taken up again, piecework which added a meagre sum to her meagre annuity. "I wish I had not promised Father to qualify as a lawyer."

"It was his dying wish, dearest, that you should not be a poor schoolmaster all your life, as he was. Think how well we shall live once you are a solicitor . . . but not with an expensive wife."

"You need not fret, Mother. I've only seen her once, and barely spoken to her. In the unlikely event that she accepted my proposal, her father certainly would not. But at least I shall see her once more. She asked where to find me so as to return my coat."

Mrs. Dinsmuir glanced around her clean, tidy, but sadly humble dwelling in alarm. "She will not come here?"

"No, I told her Wadham College. Come to think of it, she will no doubt send a footman with my coat."

"Very likely, dearest. What became of your hat?"

"It floated off down the river," Alan admitted with a sheepish look. "Stupidly, I didn't take it off before I plunged in. I'll have to make do with the old one for now, and look about the secondhand shops in town."

That reminded him of the curiosity shop, and the present he had bought for her birthday. Unless it had fallen out of his pocket in the river, Lady Beatrice would find the parcel and return it with his coat, but with no sense of urgency. Too late now to buy something else.

"Mother, I had something for your birthday, but it was in my coat pocket . . ."

"I am far too old to celebrate birthdays, dearest. But it was a kind thought, and I thank you. Go and change now, before you catch a chill," Mrs. Dinsmuir urged. "Your things will dry in the garden before you have to go back to Wadham."

Alan went up to his cubbyhole under the eaves, across from his mother's slightly larger chamber. Here he kept the tattered clothes he wore for gardening. He changed and took his wet things down to drape over a bush in the back garden, then he did some weeding. When his mother called that the kettle was boiling for tea, he pulled a few radishes and took them in.

She always had fresh tealeaves when he came, though he knew she would reuse them more than once. He suspected the bread and radishes they ate with their tea would be her last meal of the day. As a Scholar, he would eat a good dinner, for his room and board were provided by his college during the term. When he graduated in June, he would lose that. The pitiful salary he expected to earn during the required three years as an articled clerk would scarcely make up for it.

No, he had nothing to offer Lady Beatrice.

After tea, Mrs. Dinsmuir sat down by the open front window and took up her sewing again. "Read to me for a while before you go," she requested. "There is light enough, these long evenings."

*"The Arabian Nights?"* he asked with a smile, going to the bookshelf.

"Yes, let us have one of the voyages of Sindbad the Sailor." At a sound outside, she glanced out of the window. "Oh, who can this be?"

Alan joined her. A plump young woman in grey calico and a plain chipstraw bonnet was coming down the path to the front door. As she raised her hand to knock, Alan opened the door.

"Can I help you, miss?"

She looked him up and down and said doubtfully, "Be you Mr. Dinsmuir? Mr. Alan Dinsmuir."

Wishing he had changed out of his gardening clothes, even if the others were still damp, Alan said, "I am. What can I do for you, miss?"

For answer, she turned and hurried back towards the gate, calling, "It's him, my lady, it's him right enough!"

In consternation, Alan backed into the cottage, madly trying to smooth his hair with his hand.

Out in the lane, Bea's footman handed her down from the barouche. "Bring the parcels, Ephraim," she ordered.

CHERRY TREE COTTAGE read the sign on the gate. Passing her maid with a murmur of thanks, Bea trod firmly up the garden path. The well-kept garden was full of gay tulips, candytuft, sweet williams, and columbines. A rambler rose with swelling buds climbed the tiny thatched cottage, its leaves glossy against the whitewashed wall.

Bea scarcely noticed. She was concentrating on not appearing as nervous as she felt.

The proper thing to do would have been to send a footman to return Mr. Dinsmuir's coat and the odd object she found in its pocket. It was not that she wanted to see him again, she told herself. That instant of world-shaking communication between them must surely have been pure fancy. But she could not count on a footman to explain properly about the hats.

She glanced back. Yes, Ephraim had all three parcels, the two big ones and the little one, rewrapped when the soggy paper tore.

When she turned her head again, Mr. Dinsmuir stood in the doorway. The clothes he now wore were not merely shabby, but ragged and grubby, Bea saw in dismay, glad she had worn her simplest gown, blue-sprigged white muslin with a blue sash at the high waist. His face was the same, though, except that his hair had dried to light brown. His eyes were brown, too—she had been too stunned to notice the colour before. This time there was no shock, just a feeling of warm, comfortable recognition.

Gladly she saw his embarrassment fade, felt her own ebb. Smiling, he bowed.

"Good evening, Lady Beatrice. I didn't expect to see you here."

"I went first to Wadham College. The porter told me you were out, and directed me hither to your mother's house."

"Alan," came a voice from within, "do not keep the young lady standing on the doorstep, pray."

Seeing his uncertainty, Bea said, "Will you not present me to Mrs. Dinsmuir? I must tell her how her son so nobly rescued my poor Miss Dirdle."

"How is the lady?" he asked hurriedly, stepping aside to allow her to enter.

"Perfectly well, but she has retired to her bed as a precaution. Against what, I am not perfectly sure!"

As her eyes adjusted to the dimmer light inside, Bea saw a tall woman in black, who rose and came to meet her. Her brown hair, neatly banded, was scarcely touched with grey. She could not be more than fifty, while Alan appeared to be in his mid-twenties, older than most undergraduates.

"Mother, Lady Beatrice . . . Good lord, I don't know your surname!" said Mr. Dinsmuir as the ladies curtsied to each other. "How odd!"

Heartened by this evidence that he felt the same sense of long-standing familiarity, Bea said, "Albrough is my family name, ma'am."

"Hinksey's the title," said a loud, disapproving voice behind her. "The Most Honourable, the Marquis of Hinksey."

"Thank you, Ephraim," snapped Bea in annoyance. "Put the parcels on that table, if you please, and then you may go back to the carriage."

"I didn't ought to leave your ladyship alone in here," the footman said obstinately.

"Don't be tottyheaded! Molly will stay with me, not that I have any need of her. Do as I say." As Ephraim reluctantly obeyed, Bea moved to the scrubbed white-wood table. "Mrs. Dinsmuir, I have brought back the coat your son lent me. I do hope it has not shrunk. Molly, have you scissors to cut the string?"

"I didn't bring none, my lady."

Mrs. Dinsmuir said quickly, "I shall untie the knots in a trice." She set to work on the large, flat parcel.

Realizing that string was a valuable commodity in this household, Bea stripped off her gloves and reached for the top knot on the bulky, odd-shaped package.

"What is that?" asked Mr. Dinsmuir. "All you had of mine was my coat, and that." He indicated the small parcel, but as he made no move to untie it, Bea did not comment on its curious contents.

"However, you lost something else, I think," she said as the knot loosened.

"My hat, entirely through my own carelessness."

She smiled at him. "Entirely through your chivalrous haste. There." She folded back the paper to reveal a stack of top hats, nested one inside the next. "Not knowing what would fit you, I brought one of Papa's, one an uncle once left behind, and three of Cousin Tom's—one new and two grown-out-of."

"That's very kind of you," he said gruffly, taking the largest.

"You must not suppose I intend to leave you with a

cast-off. It is for emergency wear. I shall buy you a new one as soon as . . . Oh!" She clapped her hand to her mouth to stifle a giggle. "Oh, dear, even that is too small. You must have a great deal more brains than Papa."

The hat perched precariously on his head, he grinned at her. "I shall have to make do with my gardening hat for the present," he said.

"Here is your coat, Alan," said Mrs. Dinsmuir. "It looks none the worse for wear. Try it on."

"Excuse me a moment, Lady Beatrice." Taking the coat, he turned towards the stairs.

"Don't go," Bea said. "I have seen you in your shirtsleeves already and am none the worse for it. Change coats here."

So he pulled off his tattered coat and put on the other—struggled into it, rather. It was tight across the shoulders and the sleeves were now a good four inches too short. As he stood there with his arms sticking out like a scarecrow and the too small hat wobbling on his head, Bea tried desperately not to laugh.

Her eyes met his, and the laugh escaped, and it was all right because he laughed, too, and in that moment she knew she was going to marry him. What if he was a poor scholar? Papa was already furious with her, had dragged her down to the country in the middle of the Season, because she had rejected a duke's heir. Besides the sheer folly of her behaviour, half the *Beau Monde* thought he had not come up to scratch. Either way it was a delicious scandal, and Bea was in disgrace. Her father could not be any more furious because she accepted a nobody. Somehow he must be won over.

She had not the least doubt that, given the proper encouragement, Mr. Dinsmuir would propose.

"Well, Mother," he said now, "since you have a clown at hand to assist in the festivities, let me present your birthday present." With a bow made awkward by the tight coat, he handed over the little package.

"Is it your birthday, ma'am?" Bea asked as Mrs. Dinsmuir untied the knot. "May I wish you many happy returns?"

"Thank you, my dear. Oh, Alan, just like Aladdin's lamp in the picture! How splendid! Wherever did you find it?"

"In a shop in town. It's badly in need of cleaning, I'm afraid. I meant to polish it before giving it to you." Taking the lamp from her, he picked up the paper it had been wrapped in and rubbed at the verdigris.

A sound like a rushing wind filled the room, and a sharp, cold scent which made Bea think of darkness and unimaginable distances. She and the Dinsmuirs all recoiled as a column of swirling mist arose in their midst and began to coalesce into something huge and dark.

Unable to tear her eyes from the apparition, Bea felt for Mr. Dinsmuir's hand, found it, and clung.

The Jinnee was immense, his turbaned head bent beneath the low ceiling. "I was asleep," he said in a voice like thunder with a distinctly pettish undertone. "What do you want?"

# TWO

With a piercing shriek, Molly fainted. Bea hurried to tend to her maid, a crumpled heap in the corner. She knelt beside the girl, trying to make her more comfortable while not losing sight of the magical monster. In a moment Alan's mother joined her, with a bowl of water and a cloth to bathe Molly's face. Mrs. Dinsmuir, too, kept glancing over her shoulder.

Meanwhile, Mr. Dinsmuir addressed the creature. If he had lost his wits in his surprise, it had not been for long.

"For a start," he said with commendable composure, "please reduce your size if you can, and the volume of your voice. You are frightening the ladies."

"Sorry," muttered the Jinnee, shrinking rapidly until he was merely a tall, robust man. He forgot to adjust the size of his clothes, so that the smoke-grey robes draped in folds on the ground and the turban fell down over his fiery coal-black eyes. "Damn!" The garments contracted to fit.

"And don't swear in front of ladies," Mr. Dinsmuir admonished him.

"All right, all right. Did you wake me from centuries of sleep just to find fault? What can I do for you? You don't want me to repeat all that stuff about being the slave of the lamp et cetera, do you? You seem to know what's what."

"I'm familiar with the story of your association with Aladdin. Incidentally, he was a Chinaman and the story is Arabian, so how is it you speak English?"

"By the Great Roc, how should I know? Magic is magic."

"Hmm," mused Mr. Dinsmuir, "I wonder . . ."

"Look here, O Master," said the Jinnee with a touch of sarcasm, "I have no objection to your wondering, but if you want me to accomplish some task for you, perhaps I could get on with it while you wonder?"

"By all means. I'd like new clothes."

"*I'd like* . . . What sort of order is that?"

"Bring new clothes!" cried Mr. Dinsmuir. "And stop arguing!"

The Jinnee vanished.

Molly weakly raised her head. "Oh, my lady, what was that monster?" she whispered.

The Jinnee reappeared, as large as before, bumping his head on the ceiling. "Ouch!"

Molly promptly fainted again. Before her eyes were quite shut, the Jinnee had shrunk, remembering his clothes this time. At the same moment, Mr. Dinsmuir's coat, shirt, breeches and the too-small top hat he still wore turned into a long robe of green silk embroidered in gold thread and a white turban with an emerald glittering in its folds.

Bea had just time to decide he looked most impressive. Then she found herself swathed in draperies and peering out between a head shawl and a veil which covered all of her face but the eyes. Mrs. Dinsmuir was similarly enveloped, but for the veil. Molly—

"Gracious heavens!" Bea pulled the shawl from her

head and flung it over the transparent gauze which revealed most, if not quite all, of the maid's charms.

"*English* clothes!" bellowed Mr. Dinsmuir. "Please," he went on in a voice taut with self-control, "bring English clothes in the present style for my mother and me, and restore Lady Beatrice and her servant to their own attire."

"Really? Pity, that slave girl is worth a second look."

"Really!"

"No need to shout, I'm doing my best. There, is that better?"

Mr. Dinsmuir was now attired in a bottle-green morning coat which might have been fitted by Weston; a ruffled shirt, and a snowy cravat expertly tied with an emerald glittering in its folds; a biscuit-coloured waistcoat and Inexpressibles; Hessians with that shine only displayed by the finest leather; and a glossy beaver, curly-brimmed, which he hastily doffed and set on the table.

If he had been impressive in Eastern garb, he was now complete to a shade, an elegant figure fit to mix with the most fashionable gentlemen of the Fashionable World. And with the ladies, too, thought Bea, relieved at the reappearance of her sprig muslin. Mrs. Dinsmuir was the very picture of a handsome, well-bred widow, in black silk and jet beads, with a frilly, beribboned cap on her head.

"Excellent," said Mr. Dinsmuir.

"I must 'a' bin dreaming," said Molly, sitting up in her grey calico.

"*Not* a slave girl, by the way, Jinnee. As Lord Chief Justice Mansfield decided in 1772 in the case of the negro Somerset, slavery cannot exist in England."

"Is that so!" said the Jinnee in surprise. "Where

does that leave me, I wonder? I'd better get back to Headquarters and find out."

He started to fade. Bea found it somehow even more disconcerting than his previous abrupt disappearance. Molly squawked and buried her face in her hands.

"Wait!" Mr. Dinsmore commanded. "First bring us a meal, if you please, a feast fit for a birthday celebration."

"That's more like it," the Jinnee approved. "I hear and obey, O Master."

He vanished. When he returned an instant later, he remembered to keep his size reduced, but the circular tray he bore was as vast as if he were still a giant. Ignoring the table, he set it on the floor, then looked round in a dissatisfied way. He snapped his fingers, and around the tray appeared three plump cushions, covered in brocade in glowing reds and blues, with gold fringes and tassels.

The Jinnee frowned, still not quite satisfied. Again he snapped his fingers. Bea found herself kneeling on carpet instead of stone. Though nothing in the room had discernibly moved, the floor was now covered by a superb Persian rug, a Tree-of-Life design interwoven with birds and flowers.

"If there's nothing else for the moment," said the Jinnee, "I'll be off. Just rub if you want me." With a wave, he rapidly faded out of existence.

"Is he gone?" asked Molly, cautiously lowering her hands.

"Yes," Bea assured her. "I hope he is not gone for good, Mr. Dinsmuir. Loath though one must be to profit from slavery, perhaps you should have kept him in ignorance until your future affluence was assured."

"Perhaps I was a trifle precipitate," he admitted rue-fully.

"We shall do very well, dearest," said his mother. "Why, the carpet alone is of great value, and just look at the tray and the dishes on it. They are all gold and silver, and you may be sure it is not mere plate. Recall the story of Aladdin! We may live in luxury until you are admitted as a solicitor, or in comfort for many years."

All very well, thought Bea, but it was not enough to persuade her father to let her marry Alan. With a sigh, she quoted another of Miss Dirdle's favoured maxims, "No use crying over spilt milk."

"None at all," Mrs. Dinsmuir agreed. "Will you dine with us, Lady Beatrice? There is plenty for your maid, too, I am sure. Alan, help me put the dishes on the table."

"Oh no," said Bea, "it will be more fun sitting on the cushions in the Eastern style, like a picnic, if you will not be uncomfortable, ma'am. Molly, pray go and tell Ephraim and Coachman to go to the inn in the village and get something to eat. Here is a crown for them. They may pick us up in an hour."

"If you please, my lady, I'll go, too. Not a bite o' that witched food'll pass my lips," the maid said omi-nously, "not if it was everso."

"As you choose. But don't say a word of what has happened."

"Likely no one'd believe me anyways, my lady. Think I'm moon-addled, they would. I'll keep mum." She bobbed a curtsy and left.

Mrs. Dinsmuir denying the possibility of discomfort, they all took their places on the cushions. The intri-cately chased gold tray was a good four feet across, crowded with silver bowls and platters, flagons and goblets. All the dishes were covered, some with silver domes, some with damask napkins.

When Alan lifted the dome nearest him, cinnamon-scented steam arose from a concoction of saffron rice and lamb, studded with currants and pistachio nuts. Mrs. Dinsmuir found a stew of meat and apricots, while the crisp, layered pie before Bea turned out to contain chicken and eggs, sweetened, with onions and mixed spices. There were various vegetables, recognizable and exotic, some stuffed, some pickled. Quinces and apples rubbed shoulders with pomegranates and small orange fruits which—by the stones—must be fresh dates. Flat bread and oddly flavoured pastes, tarts, and fritters: more food than ought reasonably to fit on the tray.

The flagons contained wine, fruit sherbets, and something which smelled like sour milk.

"I daresay it is intended to be sour," said Bea doubtfully, bravely taking a sip. "Everything else is perfectly presented, if a trifle strange."

"A trifle!" Alan exclaimed. "It's not quite the birthday feast I had in mind for you, Mother. I'm sorry."

"Nonsense, dearest, most dishes are simply delicious."

"Think of it as an adventure, Alan," Bea suggested. Blushing as she realized she had used his Christian name, she went on hurriedly, "Just the thing for a birthday surprise, even if one will be quite content to return to roast beef and green peas tomorrow. Beef in one form or another is always my cousin Tom's first choice. But perhaps you prefer mutton, or ham, Mr. Dinsmuir?"

"I prefer 'Alan,' Lady Beatrice," he said softly.

"Oh!" Her face flaming, she stammered, "My family and friends call me Bea, two syllables, Be-a, not bee like a bumblebee. Oh dear, I am babbling. But will you, please . . . ?"

"Of course, Bea dear," said Mrs. Dinsmuir kindly, though she seemed rather dismayed, "if you are truly sure you wish it."

"I do." The unintended echo of the marriage service further disconcerted her. She peeped at Alan.

He said nothing, but the besotted bliss on his face was enough. Their fingers met and intertwined.

The door knocker sounded. "Is that there monster in there?" came Molly's voice. "I'll wait out here for you, my lady."

"Have I been here so long?" cried Bea, jumping up. "Mama will be wondering where I am. I shall be shockingly late for dinner and unable to eat a bite. I am coming, Molly."

"Wait a minute." Rising, Alan reached for the lamp. "If I have not ruined everything, the Jinnee will transport you home in a trice."

Bea shook her head, half regretfully, half in relief. "It will not do. I hope I am not so poor-spirited as to be afraid of rushing through the ether, but Molly would die of fright—and so might the horses! Also, if Ephraim and Coachman find out about the Jinnee, everyone will soon know. I think it best that Papa does not discover what means you use to . . . to . . ." She stopped, having worked herself into an inextricable position.

"To turn myself into an eligible suitor," Alan said soberly. "It will take some doing, even with the Jinnee's help. Without, it may prove impossible."

"We shall manage, somehow. Mrs. Dinsmuir, may I call upon you tomorrow afternoon?"

The widow sighed. "Yes, dear. I can only hope the two of you know what you are about. Alan . . ."

"My lady?" Molly called nervously.

"Coming." Bea looked up at Alan.

Tenderly his lips brushed hers. "Until tomorrow, darling Bea." He went to open the door.

Alan watched from the threshold until Bea disappeared behind the hedge. Then he listened to the thud of hooves, jingle of harness, and creak of wheels, fading away until a robin's song rang louder. He turned and went into the cottage.

His mother had lit a tallow candle and moved two dishes from the tray on the floor to the table. As she returned for more, he caught her by the waist in a big hug, lifting her inches off the floor.

"She loves me!"

"Put me down, Alan! I agree that Lady Beatrice appears to have taken a liking to you, but I put no faith in such sudden attraction. Very likely she will think better of it tonight and not turn up tomorrow."

Alan hardly heard a word. "Is she not wonderful?" he demanded, attempting to lift the tray. Failing, he helped to transfer the dishes to the table. "When the Jinnee appeared, her first concern was to succor that widgeon of a maidservant, though I know she also was terrified, for she clutched my hand." He laid said hand against his cheek and stood for a moment in rapt contemplation.

"A very pretty-behaved young lady," Mrs. Dinsmuir concurred, "but a *Lady*, and far above your touch, dearest."

"Not with the aid of the Slave of the Lamp, Mother."

"Whom you have released from his bondage."

"I could not do otherwise. The law is the law." Alan dropped despondently onto a chair and sat with his chin in his hand, gazing at the window, outside which dusk was gathering. "Perhaps he will continue to serve me out of gratitude."

"The Jinn in the stories are not noted for their gratitude upon release," his mother pointed out, busy combining the leftover food in a few dishes and setting the empty ones aside to be washed. "Have you forgot the story of the fisherman who freed the Jinnee from the bottle and as a reward was nearly done to death?"

"That was an Afreet, an evil Jinnee. Ours is one of the good ones. I think. I wonder, if we used the proceeds of selling this gold and silver to go to America, to one of the slave states, would he be bound to serve the owner of the lamp again? I could have him amass a fortune for me there, then come back and woo Bea— or rather Lord Hinksey—in proper form."

"It would scarcely be fair to her to ask her to wait for so uncertain an outcome, dearest."

"She will wait," Alan said confidently. "She loves me. Still, perhaps it won't be necessary. I'll see if the Jinnee will answer my summons. Where is the . . . But I keep forgetting, Mother, the lamp is yours, not mine."

"It is the person who holds it, not who owns it, that counts. I shall not give it back, because it is quite the most exciting birthday present ever given me, but I am perfectly content to let you do the rubbing!" She found the green-tarnished lamp among the gleaming silver dishes and handed it to him. "Otherwise, I should take some sand to it and give it a good polishing."

"Let that be his first task," said Alan, laughing in spite of his suspense, "if he comes."

Heart in mouth, he rubbed his knuckles across the lamp.

A gale, heard and sensed rather than felt, swept through the room, disturbing not a hair on their heads. A tang like the smell of sea brine made Alan think of small ships setting out across vast, uncharted oceans. Above the table between him and his mother, a column of writhing mist began to form.

As its top reached the ceiling, a pair of flaming black eyes glowered through the haze. "To the deuce with this furniture-fixated society," grumbled an irritable voice.

The mist hopped down to the floor and solidified into the Jinnee, in his large but manageable form.

"At your bidding I come, O Master," he announced unnecessarily. "What is your command?"

"Does this mean you are still slave to whoever holds the lamp?" Alan asked.

"Not exactly. I'm a free Jinnee as long as the lamp is in a free country, but it seems I inadvertently engaged myself to serve you. An implied contract, they call it. A quarter's notice on either side, and I hereby give notice. From your point of view, the catch is that you have to pay me for the next three months."

"Pay you what?"

"It's for you to make an offer, for me to accept or refuse." He grinned cheekily. "There is one stipulation: my wages cannot consist of anything I myself have provided."

"You will not . . ." Mrs. Dinsmuir faltered, ". . . you will not kill him if he fails to propose a suitable salary?"

The Jinnee drew himself up to his full height, incautiously growing until his head hit the ceiling. "Ouch! Madam, do I look like an Afreet?" he enquired, affronted.

"Not in the least," she hastily assured him. "That is the second time you have knocked your head. Is it sore? I have some comfrey balm which is excellent for bruises."

"Most kind!" The Jinnee was restored to good humour. Indeed, he looked quite gratified. "My turban protected me, madam, but I do appreciate your sympathy. By the Great Roc, no mortal has ever before proposed to do anything for *me!*"

"I should very much like to do something for you," Alan broke in, "to wit, to pay you an appropriate wage. However, so far I have racked my brains in vain. Do the rules allow me to request your own suggestions?"

"Good question. I have no notion. I had best go and enquire."

As he began to fade, Mrs. Dinsmuir reached out to touch his sleeve. "Before you go, Mr. Jinnee," she said, "I have one very small favour to ask. Will you be offended if I say the state of your lamp is unworthy of so powerful a being?"

"I have often thought so myself, madam. *My* lamp, you say? To be sure, it belongs to me more than to its temporary possessors. Unfortunately, I cannot clean it without an order, and none have given me such an order."

He looked hopefully at Alan, who still held the lamp. Alan obliged. "Please polish it."

In a twinkling, the lamp gleamed coppery in the candlelight. The Jinnee beamed. "Thank you," he said.

"Thank *you,*" said Mrs. Dinsmuir.

"My pleasure, madam. Do you know, I cannot see the need to trouble Headquarters again in so small a matter. What I should like, sir," he continued, almost shyly, "is to live with you as your servant, instead of having to dash here from the back of beyond whenever you summon me. I have never had an opportunity to observe the mortal world at leisure, just those bits and pieces I happen to catch sight of when on an errand."

"And that would be reward enough for your service?" Alan asked in surprise, and some dismay, eyeing the still massive figure in his turban, robe, and billowing trousers.

"Why not? Think about it: For millennia I've been at the beck and call of any fool who happens to pick up my lamp." As he stressed the possessive, he cast an approving look at Mrs. Dinsmuir. "It's been 'Come here. Do this, do that, do the other. All right, we don't need you anymore, off you go to the nether world and kindly don't reappear until you're summoned.' Positively demeaning, when you consider it."

"Most unfair," Mrs. Dinsmuir said warmly.

"You would not mind, Mother? Having the . . . gentleman about the place?"

"Not a bit, dearest. I daresay Mr. Jinnee would not mind giving a hand with the housework now and then."

A trifle taken aback, the Jinnee glanced about the kitchen-parlour. "Surely, sir, you will not remain in this place—charming as it is, madam," he put in hastily—"now that I am here to serve you. A palace, with a large staff, can be yours in the twinkling of an eye."

"Now wait a bit!" Alan exclaimed. "Let us not be too precipitate. This is going to take a great deal of thought. I must consult Bea as to the best way to win her father's consent to our marriage. Her father is a marquis, you see, Jinnee, and I am naught but a poor scholar."

"Aha!" said the Jinnee. "So that's the way of it. I suspected something of the sort. A delightful young lady, if I may be so bold, sir, though far from modestly dressed."

"She was perfectly modestly dressed," Alan said hotly (much of the heat coming from a sudden memory of Bea emerging from the Cherwell, naiadlike, in skin-clinging, near-transparent muslin), "for this time and place. Which brings me to the question of your attire, Jinnee. If you wish to become part of the household, you will need to wear clothes that are rather . . . er . . . less remarkable, so as to avoid gossip."

"You don't expect me to wear one of those strangling things around my neck, do you?" the Jinnee asked in horror.

"A cravat. Yes."

"And tight trousers? And no turban?"

"I'm afraid so. And if you could reduce your size a little more, it would help."

The Jinnee heaved a long, gusty sigh. As he exhaled, he shrank, until his eyes were exactly on a level with Alan's, though he remained considerably bulkier. At the same time, his robe and voluminous trousers metamorphosed until he was properly garbed for an upper servant—except for the turban.

"No turban?" he asked wistfully.

"Let him keep it, Alan," urged his mother. "People will just assume he is an Indian. I am sure India nabobs sometimes bring back native servants to England."

"Very well, at least for the present." Alan found he

was too tired after an emotionally exhausting day to consider the extraordinary situation from every angle. All he wanted was to be alone to hug to himself the knowledge that Bea loved him.

*"Thank* you, sir."

"We shall see tomorrow what Bea thinks about the turban. Jinnee, I must return to college tonight, but you had best remain here, or you are free to go home—if that is the appropriate word—if you wish. Mother, I'm off. I'll be back in the morning after chapel."

He kissed her cheek and turned towards the door. Before he reached it, he found himself flying through the night sky. Bright stars twinkled above, and as he swooped down Headington Hill the twinkling lights of Oxford came into sight below. He swept over the gleaming ribbon of the Cherwell. An instant later he was standing in his study-bedroom in Wadham College.

Catching his breath, which he had held for the entire journey, so short a time had it taken, Alan dropped into a chair. He had not ordered the Jinnee to bring him here. If his new servant, with his shaky understanding of modern English life, had decided to lend a helpful hand without awaiting instructions, only trouble could ensue!

# THREE

Bea lay awake half the night. Part of the time she luxuriated in loving and knowing she was loved. Part of the time she wondered whether Alan Dinsmuir could possibly be as wonderful as she remembered him. And part of the time she wondered whether a gentleman so clever as to make a serious study of the law could possibly truly love anyone so frivolous as her unworthy self.

Being young, she rose in the morning showing no sign of her restless vigil. On the contrary, she was full of confidence, determination, and energy.

The energy demanded an immediate outlet. After a large breakfast with her father—she responded with sunny smiles to Papa's ominous mutterings about girls who turned down the heirs to dukedoms coming to regret their folly and ending up as old maids—Bea set off across the park to climb Hinksey Hill.

It was another beautiful day, the air crystal clear. Though no great prominence, the hill afforded an excellent view of the city of Oxford. Bea had brought a map of the city and her father's spyglass. Seated on the dry turf, she amused herself with trying to pick out the buildings of Wadham College.

Alan must finish his degree, she thought. He only

had a few weeks to go. Who could tell when it might be useful?

Papa might prove obdurate. Lowering the glass, Bea surveyed the vast Palladian mansion below, and sighed. She supposed it was natural that the owner of Hinksey Hall would refuse to let his only child wed a threadbare scholar whose home was a tiny cottage. With the Jinnee's continued help, which was by no means certain, Alan would cease to be a threadbare scholar, but he would still lack a noble family.

And what if something went wrong, as it did with Aladdin, whose wife and palace had vanished overnight? He had recovered them with the aid of a magic ring, but Alan had no such alternative Jinnee to call upon.

Bea had some money of her own, fifteen thousand pounds she would come into on her twenty-first birthday. It sounded like a lot of money, if one did not spend hundreds of guineas on ball dresses and such extravagances. However, she had not the least notion whether it would suffice for three people to live on in modest comfort. Better to consider it a supplement to Alan's earnings.

"Gracious, how practical I am growing!" she said aloud with a little laugh.

"I beg your pardon, my lady?" said a familiar voice behind her.

"Oh!" Bea swung round, hand to thudding heart. "How you startled me, Jinnee." Taking in his changed appearance, she went on doubtfully, "You are Mr. Dinsmuir's Jinnee, are you not?"

"After a fashion, my lady," he said, bowing. "I apologize for startling your ladyship. Mr. Dinsmuir and I have come to an agreement over the terms of my ser-

vice, but it was Mrs. Dinsmuir who sent me to speak
to your ladyship. Madam is most concerned lest the
master has misled himself in attributing your ladyship's kindness to—ahem—warmer feelings."

Bea blushed. "No. You may tell Mrs. Dinsmuir that
I am quite determined to marry her son. That is, if
he . . ."

"Your ladyship may rest assured that the master
is . . . 'heels over head' was the expression madam
used, I believe. Madam affirms that a mother cannot
be wrong in such cases. I must say, the lad looked to
me pretty far gone," the Jinnee added confidentially.

Throwing her arms around him, Bea stood on tiptoe to kiss his swarthy cheek, which promptly turned
a dusky pink.

"We'll bring your father round, never fear," he said
in a gruff voice.

At that moment, the church bells in the village began to ring for the morning service. "Bother, I shall
be late for church," Bea said. "See, the carriage is
already at the door. Mama will be in high fidgets."

"I'll take you down," offered the Jinnee.

Before Bea had time to accept or refuse, she was
whisked through the air, and before she had time to
gasp in shock, she was set down gently behind a pillar
on the front steps.

"Not far enough to get up a good speed," the Jinnee's voice grumbled in her ear. She spun around,
but he was invisible. "I shall return to Mrs. Dinsmuir,"
he said. "Until later."

In a thoughtful mood, Bea went down the steps to
the carriage. By luck or good management, no one
seemed to have observed her whirlwind arrival. Nonetheless, the notion that the Jinnee had not awaited an

order, or even a request, alarmed her. What might he take it into his head to do next?


After church, Bea persuaded Miss Dirdle that she really ought to call on the mother of the young gentleman who had saved her from drowning.

Bea did not want to take Molly with her. The maid had convinced herself that yesterday's horrid apparition was the result of eating something which disagreed with her. Best to leave her with that belief.

Miss Dirdle, on the other hand, had introduced Bea to the *Arabian Nights* tales in childhood. A confirmed romantic at heart, the governess had sighed longingly over the exotic settings and magical happenings, and especially over the happily-ever-after love stories. What was more, she sympathized with Bea's refusal to marry a man she did not love, however exalted his station.

Hoping her dear Miss Dirdle would sympathize equally with her desire to marry a man she *did* love, however humble his station, Bea set out with her companion in the barouche.

They drove through the city and across Magdalen Bridge. Miss Dirdle shuddered at the sight of the peaceable stream which had so nearly claimed her life.

"Indeed, I owe Mr. Dinsmuir my hearty gratitude," she affirmed. "You are right, my dear, though naturally one cannot call upon a gentleman; one may hope to encounter him at his esteemed parent's abode, and there to express one's thanks."

As they started up Headington Hill, Bea caught sight of a figure ahead of them, striding along the high, embanked footpath beside the road. Though last time she saw Alan walking away from her he had been shabby and soaking wet, she would have recognized him anywhere. Her heart gave an odd little jump, and she ordered the coachman to stop beside him.

"Mr. Dinsmuir," she said breathlessly, gazing up at his beloved face, high above her, "may we offer you a lift?"

"My dear Lady Beatrice," he said, his obvious elation on seeing her giving way to a grin, "the very sight of you lifts my heart so high, I am afraid of knocking my head against the sky. But if you will have your coachman move along to the next steps, I shall be delighted to come down and . . . Good Lord, what on earth?"

He turned and stared up the hill.

Bea became aware of an approaching clamour, dogs barking, boys cheering. She stood up and peered past the coachman.

"Looks like the circus is coming to town, my lady," he observed, pointing with his whip.

He had to put it down suddenly, as the racket made the horses sidle nervously. Bea knelt on the forward seat and steadied herself with a hand on its back.

Down the hill came an extraordinary procession. In the lead, at a stately pace, came a beautiful girl in a robe embroidered with gold and studded with jewels. On her head she balanced a golden bowl covered with gold brocade, also gem-studded, glittering in the sunshine. At her side walked a plump African in voluminous white trousers, a brief jacket open down the front, and a turban. Behind them came another couple, just the same, and another, and another . . .

"Jinnee!" swore Alan.

Scrambling, he lowered himself from the embankment onto the barouche seat beside Bea, stepped to the floor, and thence sprang to the ground. While Bea collapsed in helpless giggles and Miss Dirdle sat open-mouthed, he ran to the first eunuch slave.

"Stop!" he shouted.

Without pausing in his pace, the African answered with a stream of liquid, incomprehensible syllables. The Jinnee's magic translation effect apparently only worked for him in person.

Alan stepped in front of the front pair, arms spread wide. The column simply parted to flow around him. The parade continued down the hill towards the city.

Hurrying back to the barouche, Alan jumped in. "Go on, Coachman," he cried, "and make haste!"

"Yes, do," Bea seconded him, as the coachman turned to her for orders. She no longer felt like laughing. In a lower voice she said to Alan, "I dread to think what Papa will do if they reach Hinksey Hall."

"I'll have that Jinnee's blood!" Alan vowed vengefully.

"If he has anything as mundane as blood in his veins. But, darling, he is just trying to help us. That is exactly what he did for Aladdin to win the Sultan's consent, is it not, Miss Dirdle?"

"Aladdin?" said Miss Dirdle in confusion. "Really, Lady Beatrice, I cannot conceive . . ."

"My apologies, ma'am," Alan said. "You must think us fit for Bedlam. Indeed, you may be right. My brain is in a whirl." He clutched at his head. "Bea, you had better explain."

"First, let me introduce you properly. Miss Dirdle, this is Alan Dinsmuir, the gentleman who fished you out of the Cherwell yesterday."

Miss Dirdle's effusive thanks took them the rest of

the way up the hill. The barouche turned off the main road, and Bea had time for only a brief explanation, which left Miss Dirdle more confused than enlightened, before they reached Mrs. Dinsmuir's cottage.

With a grim "Excuse me, ladies," Alan sped through the gate in the hedge, shouting, "Where's that Jinnee?"

The footman who jumped down from the step at the back to hand down the ladies was not the disapproving Ephraim, Bea had made sure of that. Reuben used to smuggle her sugarplums when she was in disgrace as a child. She swore him and Coachman to secrecy, sent them off to the inn for a pint of ale, then preceded an apprehensive Miss Dirdle up the garden path.

The cottage looked bigger. Not conspicuously, with an extra wing, or storey, or even more windows—just as if it had been stretched in all directions. The impression was confirmed when Bea stepped in through the open door. The ceiling was higher. The kitchen area had vanished behind a partition. The remaining space easily accommodated the table and rush-bottom chairs she recalled, as well as a set of low, comfortably cushioned divans, where before three cushions on the floor had scarcely fitted.

No sign of Alan, nor of the Jinnee. No raised voices. Bea clasped Mrs. Dinsmuir's hands, held out to her as she entered.

"What has he done, ma'am? What have they done?" Bea asked anxiously.

"What happened? What has Alan in such a miff?" his mother asked at the same moment. "He dashed in here, raging, and commanded Mr. Jinnee to take him into town at once."

"Oh, dear, was the Jinnee offended? I do hope Alan will remember how powerful he is, and be tactful. He did not harm him, or threaten him?"

"Certainly not!" said Mrs. Dinsmuir, quite sharply. "Mr. Jinnee is a charming and most obliging gentleman. I do not know what he did to make Alan angry, but I am perfectly certain his aim was to help."

"He does seem to *wish* to be helpful," Bea admitted.

"He told me he knew exactly the thing to make your papa look kindly upon . . . Oh!" She suddenly noticed Miss Dirdle, dithering on the threshold, and moved forward to greet her. "My dear ma'am, I am so sorry. Pray pay no heed to our nonsense. Do come in."

Bea hastily introduced them. Mrs. Dinsmuir seated her bewildered guest on one of her new divans. "You will feel the better for a cup of tea," she said soothingly. "The kettle is on the hob, it will not take a moment."

"The very thing," said Bea. "We came out straight after church, without any refreshment."

"Then you will like something to eat as well. I have some pastries, rather unusual, but quite delicious."

"I shall come and help you carry everything."

"My dear Lady Beatrice!" Miss Dirdle exclaimed, shocked.

Sitting down beside the old lady, Bea took her hands. "Miss Dirdle, Mrs. Dinsmuir is going to be my mama-in-law."

"Oh, my dear!"

"I am quite determined to marry Mr. Alan Dinsmuir, with or without Papa's permission."

"My dear child!"

"But naturally I should prefer to have his blessing,

and Mama's, so we must strive to come up with a plan to win it, with or without the Jinnee's help."

"The Jinnee?" said Miss Dirdle in a faint voice.

"Large as life, and twice as natural—or rather, natural as life and twice as large. You will help, too, will you not?" Bea pleaded.

"Of course," Miss Dirdle vowed staunchly.

"I knew I could count on you." Bea kissed her, and followed Mrs. Dinsmuir to the kitchen to fetch the tea tray.

The pastries were indeed delicious, flaky and filled with nuts and honey. Munching and sipping, the ladies discussed the situation.

First Bea described the parade. Mrs. Dinsmuir had to agree that forty black slaves and forty beautiful girls, even with gold bowls of priceless jewels on their heads, were unlikely to win the marquis's favour.

"Oh, dear, I fear Lord Hinksey—like your coachman—would imagine someone had sent the circus to call."

"And were his lordship to be persuaded to believe the gems were genuine," put in Miss Dirdle, "he would consider it mere vulgar display. I do hope Mr. Dinsmuir has succeeded in diverting the procession."

"Mr. Jinnee will see to it," Mrs. Dinsmuir said with confidence, "once he understands the impropriety of such an offering to an English nobleman."

In spite of the widow's assurances, Bea was by no means convinced that the Jinnee would not turn on Alan for scorning his enterprise. On tenterhooks, she wondered why they had not yet returned, since the Jinnee could make the entire procession disappear with a wave of his hand.

"Am I to understand, ma'am," Miss Dirdle was saying tentatively, "that the . . . the Jinnee is not a figment from Lady Beatrice's dreams? He truly exists?"

Mrs. Dinsmuir and Bea united to satisfy her doubts.

Thrilled, eyes sparkling, the ex-governess clasped her hands. "I cannot wait to meet him!"

She had quite a wait. The ladies had finished their second cups of tea and were all growing worried when at last Alan and the Jinnee materialized before them.

"Oh!" squeaked Miss Dirdle.

The Jinnee looked disgruntled. Alan dropped onto the nearest divan and mopped his brow.

"Whew," he sighed, "what a business!"

"Alan, you did catch them before they reached Papa, did you not?" Bea moved over to sit beside him.

"We caught up with them just as they crossed Magdalen Bridge, but there were far too many people watching to make them vanish."

"I had not thought. What a commotion that would have caused!"

Alan grinned. "It might have been funny, but there was quite a commotion already, and I did not dare risk a riot. All down the High they marched, with the crowds growing, until by the time we came to Carfax, the proctors and beadles had to be sent for to clear a way. Actually, a magistrate turned up and wanted them arrested for parading without a license and causing disorderly conduct, but he could not make them understand, so he gave up."

"Good gracious," said Mrs. Dinsmuir, "how very fortunate they were not locked up in the city gaol. If they had disappeared from there, I hate to think of the consequences. But whatever did you do, Alan?"

Miss Dirdle leaned forward. "Waited until they were out in the country, I expect," she suggested.

"Precisely, ma'am." Alan bowed to her and she gave him a look of approval. "No one followed very far beyond the city streets, and if the odd yokel saw them dematerialize, he would hardly believe his own eyes, far less be believed."

"Oh darling, how clever," Bea cried, gazing up at him admiringly. He looked down, and they lost themselves in each other's eyes. His mother's voice seemed to come from far away.

"Neatly done, dearest."

"Am I to understand, madam," said the Jinnee gloomily, "that you, too, disdain my efforts?"

"Disdain? Never! Your desire to assist is altogether praiseworthy, Mr. Jinnee, and I respect you for it."

"However, my dear sir," said Miss Dirdle, "undeniably, the method chosen was sadly inappropriate."

"It worked for Aladdin," he pointed out.

The two ladies did their best to soothe him, attempting to explain why a vast fortune in jewels was an unsuitable gift for a marquis. "Especially if it arrives on the heads of a column of maidens, however lovely, escorted by eunuch slaves," Mrs. Dinsmuir added.

"It makes no sense to me," the Jinnee said frankly, "but I must take your word for it. Which leaves me with the question, what do we do next to bring a happy conclusion to their love?"

The united scrutiny of the Jinnee, Mrs. Dinsmuir, and Miss Dirdle brought Bea and Alan out of their rosy haze.

"Er, what?" said Alan, with less than his usual intelligence.

"I await your commands, O master," announced the Jinnee indulgently.

"What shall we do next, dearest?" asked Mrs. Dinsmuir.

"Good Lord, I haven't the faintest idea. Bea, darling?"

"Oh Alan, I simply do not know!"

"Then listen to me," said Miss Dirdle. "I have a splendid notion!"

# FOUR

"Dash it, Bea, a *gentleman* don't come up to Oxford to study," Tom protested. "Just to knock up a few larks, and get to know the right sort of people before going on the Town."

Lord Wendover nodded.

"Then you refuse to help, because Alan is cleverer than you?" Bea asked scornfully, slashing with her riding whip at an inoffensive hedgerow. May petals flew. Her mare and Lord Wendover started.

"Nothing of the sort!" her cousin denied. "Dash it, Bea, the fellow's nobody, and you're the daughter of the Marquis of Hinksey."

Lord Wendover nodded.

"That is why we need you," Bea pointed out. "Colonel McMahon is bound at least to give you the courtesy of a hearing, as you are Papa's heir. And even more so if Lord Wendover goes with you, as he already has a title."

Lord Wendover nodded.

"Dash it, Bea, you can't expect Windy to help when he's in love with you himself."

Lord Wendover nodded.

Bea said seriously, "Lord Wendover, if I were to tell you I will marry you in three weeks' time, as soon as the banns can be read, what would you do?"

"Oh, I say, Lady Beatrice," his lordship bleated in alarm. "Not quite ready for marriage, don't you know. Desperately in love with you and all that, but I was thinking of waiting a few years."

"Well, I cannot wait, even if I wanted to marry you. I should be an old maid by then. Anyway, it is Alan Dinsmuir I want to marry. If you *truly* love me, you must want me to be happy, and I cannot be happy without Alan. I love him desperately."

"Can't see what you see in the fellow," Tom grumbled.

"He saved Miss Dirdle from drowning."

"I'd have pulled you out first, Lady Beatrice," Lord Wendover assured her.

"It was your fault she fell in," Tom reminded his friend, "but all the same, Windy's right, Bea. No gallant beau in his senses would rescue an old crow—an elderly, ill-favoured lady"—he amended hastily, catching Bea's kindling eye—"before he saved the pretty young lady."

"Precisely," said Bea.

Tom and Lord Wendover looked at each other blankly, and shrugged. "There's no understanding females," said Tom. "Maggots in their heads, the lot of them. The fact remains, Dinsmuir's nobody."

"But if Miss Dirdle's plan works, with your help, he will not be nobody," Bea said persuasively. "She says it is well known that the Prince Regent hands out titles right and left to people who 'lend' him money, without expecting repayment."

Lord Wendover nodded.

"But Dinsmuir's poor as a church mouse," Tom objected.

"Not anymore. He has come into a *vast* fortune,

quite unexpectedly, only you know Papa will not be swayed by mere wealth."

Tom was suspicious. "Where did all this rhino come from all of a sudden?"

"From the Orient," Bea said warily. The conspirators had decided to stick to the truth as far as was humanly possible.

Lord Wendover nodded, knowledgeably this time. "Long-lost uncle turned out to be an India nabob, I daresay."

"Something like that. But Alan cannot simply send Prinny a bank draught with a note asking for a title in exchange."

"Lord no!" Tom exclaimed, horrified. "They'd send him to the Tower for *lèse majesté*. You have to do the thing a bit more subtly than that, Bea, get an audience with Prinny and drop a few subtle hints, that sort of thing."

"McMahon's the chap," observed Lord Wendover. "Prinny's Private Secretary, don't you know. I say, Tom, it'd be a bit of a lark to see if we could persuade Colonel McMahon to let in a nobody like Dinsmuir to see the Prince Regent."

"Lord yes, what a caper! I wonder if he's in London now, or down in Brighton?"

Bea smiled a secret smile and listened to their plotting, putting in a word here and there to turn them from their more extravagant flights of fancy. When it came to the fantastic, the Jinnee was the best in the business.

With all the magical resources at his command, the Jinnee was disgusted by Alan's refusal to permit him to counterfeit coin of the realm. Instead, while his master conned his books and took his final examinations, the Jinnee went through a great deal of tedious—and in his view unnecessary—fuss and bother in London.

Mrs. Dinsmuir, in her widow's weeds, would arrive at a goldsmith's or dealer's premises, her turbaned servant following a pace behind. None were so distrustful or discourteous as to enquire as to the provenance of the articles of gold and silver this dark-skinned, but obviously trusted menial produced for sale. It was perfectly obvious that the lady's late husband must have been in the India service, in a most remunerative position. The righthand man of some nawab, no doubt, struck down by one of those virulent tropical fevers.

Goldsmiths and dealers were gently sympathetic, and perhaps a touch more generous than usual. The goods, after all, were of unusually pure precious metals. Mrs. Henrietta Dinsmuir opened substantial accounts at Child's Bank, Coutts' Bank, and Rothschild's Bank.

"Thus we shall avoid arousing suspicion," she explained to the Jinnee as they left the last, "besides not risking all our eggs in one basket."

"All money changers and usurers are alike," he grumbled, handing her into the carriage. He had conjured up this modest but comfortable vehicle earlier, along with horses and driver, in a secluded spot on the outskirts of the metropolis. "Far better to keep your gold in iron chests in a vault under your own control, madam."

"I wish you will not call me madam, Mr. Jinnee," she said earnestly as he took the opposite seat. "Miss Dirdle, who understands the ways of the world, advises that you should hold the position of my son's secretary, not his valet. A secretary is a gentleman, not a mere servant. As such you may properly address me by name, or at least as ma'am."

"I did not wish to presume, Henrietta."

Mrs. Dinsmuir blushed, as she had not in decades. "Not my Christian name"—she said hurriedly, then added, for she had no wish to hurt him—"or only when we are quite private."

The Jinnee positively flickered with delight. Mrs. Dinsmuir accepted this somewhat unnerving spectacle with equanimity—sometimes she was amazed at how quickly she had grown accustomed to the manifestations of magic.

They drove south into Surrey, to ensure that no one could connect the flood of gold and silver with the poor Oxford student. As soon as they were in the country, the carriage turned into a deserted lane and disappeared, horses, coachman, occupants, and all. A few seconds later, Mrs. Dinsmuir was home in her cottage again.

Meanwhile, Tom and Lord Wendover had returned from London with Colonel McMahon's consent to Mr. Dinsmuir's proposal. They were both promptly sent down for the rest of the term, for unauthorized absence from their college. Undismayed, they went straight back to Town to enjoy the amusements of the end of the Season.

As soon as Alan finished his legal studies, Bea and her governess tutored him in the proper etiquette for approaching the Prince Regent. Now they came to the cottage to wish him good luck.

"Luck!" muttered the Jinnee. "There's no need of luck with *me* to guide him."

Alan was not listening, since Bea's notion of speeding him on his way involved considerable bodily contact. Miss Dirdle's scandalized cluckings had no effect. In the end, urged by Mrs. Dinsmuir, the Jinnee plucked him bodily—or rather, magically—from his beloved's embrace. He found himself in a carriage entering London, seated next to his mother and opposite his "secretary."

"You did not let me say goodbye properly," he said indignantly.

His mother exchanged a complicitous glance with the Jinnee. "I thought that was what you were doing," she said. "Five minutes seemed to me long enough."

"It wasn't anywhere near five minutes."

"To be precise, seven minutes, forty-seven seconds," the Jinnee confirmed blandly.

"Well, it seemed more like just forty-seven seconds." Alan lapsed into a daydream in which Bea's warm, supple body was still in his arms, her sweet lips still soft as satin on his own.

He emerged from his dream to sign the papers which added his name to Mrs. Dinsmuir's various bank accounts, and others which ordered the purchase of Government Bonds. He was rich beyond his wildest dreams. Yet all the wealth of the Indies—which was, in fact, at his command through the Jinnee—meant nothing to him if it did not win him Bea's hand. And all the wealth of the Indies counted for nothing in Lord Hinksey's eyes if his daughter's suitor had no title to lend it legitimacy.

"Mother, suppose the Prince won't accept my gifts?"

"They say he is constantly at Point Non Plus, dearest."

"Suppose he considers me unworthy of being ennobled?"

"My own grandmother was the daughter of a baron, though the line has died out. You are a gentleman and the son of a gentleman."

"The son of a schoolmaster and grandson of a clergyman."

"Who was the younger son of a baronet."

"Back in the mists of time."

"The mists of time?" the Jinnee cackled. "A century or less! When you have existed for millennia, young man, you may speak of the mists of time."

Abashed, Alan gave voice to a fear he had scarcely acknowledged to himself: "Suppose everyone laughs at our entertainment?"

The Jinnee swelled with wrath until his turban touched the carriage roof. "Laugh?" he said awfully. "At *my* entertainment? I'll turn them into cockroaches!"

"That certainly would land Alan in the Tower, Mr. Jinnee," said Mrs. Dinsmuir, patting his huge brown hand soothingly. He subsided a little. "Miss Dirdle and dear Bea agree that the Prince Regent takes his oriental palace very seriously. If he chooses to stage an oriental pageant in his music room, not the slightest titter will be heard, you may depend upon it."

"All the same," Alan said with fervour, "I wouldn't go through this for anyone but Bea. I had rather slay any number of dragons."

"Is that a command, O Master?" asked the Jinnee, and rumbled with laughter at the horrified face Alan turned to him.

The carriage stopped. The Jinnee whisked Mrs. Dinsmuir home, and returned to transport Alan and his equipage to a lonely spot on the South Downs above Brighton. Sheep scattered, bleating, as the coach and four materialized in their midst. A shepherd rubbed his eyes and stared again, while his dogs barked and nipped the wheels in an effort to drive off the intruder.

It took the hint, rolling away along the chalky track, down into the wooded hollow where the London road descended towards the town.

Mr. Dinsmuir and his secretary took rooms at the first respectable inn they came to. It was no part of Miss Dirdle's plan for him to make a display of his vast wealth to anyone but the Prince Regent. Alan was relieved, but it had taken the combined efforts of Mrs. Dinsmuir and Bea to persuade the Jinnee of the necessity for reticence on the subject. He was still disgruntled.

Once settled at the inn, Alan and the Jinnee strolled into the centre of Brighton. The first sight of the Royal Pavilion stunned Alan. Studded with onion domes, spires, and minarets, the façade all slender pillars and arched windows topped with lacy stone fretwork, it looked like something straight out of the *Arabian Nights*.

The Jinnee was delighted. "By the Great Roc, that's what a royal palace should look like," he approved. "Something of the Muscovite, something of Hindostan, a touch of Baghdad, and a hint of China. Not your square, solid English piles, with the rows of square windows, and square chimneys, and columns strong enough to hold up a mountain. The prince who built this will certainly appreciate my entertainment."

"No scantily-clad dancers," Alan reminded him anxiously. "We are still in England. There will be ladies present."

"A strange custom," the Jinnee mused with a sigh, brightening as he continued, "though not without its advantages."

They found the side door to which they had been directed, and enquired for Colonel McMahon. The Regent's trusted personal aide came to them, rather than having them brought to him, and he greeted them with rather affected courtesy. Alan wondered just what his beloved's cousin had told the ugly little man in the blue and buff uniform to lead to such complaisance.

As McMahon led them into the Pavilion, Alan was too apprehensive to pay much heed to the apartments they passed through. He was aware of the Jinnee's approving grunts, but he concentrated on what the colonel was saying.

"I have been given to understand that you propose to offer an entertainment for His Royal Highness and his guests, Mr. Dinsmuir? And that in the course of the pageant, a number of . . . ah . . . *objets d'art* will be presented to His Highness?"

"Yes," Alan affirmed, continuing as tutored by Miss Dirdle, "I can think of no one who is more capable of appreciating the beauty and value of the oriental treasures in my possession. It will be a pleasure to add to the magnificent collection for which His Royal Highness is famous."

Mchahon nodded, with a cynical smile. "His Highness will assuredly find a way to express his gratitude, assuming the gifts are bestowed in a suitably . . . ah . . . decorous fashion. I shall need to know the details of your pageant in advance."

"For that, you must consult my secretary, Mr. Jinnee, who has arranged the whole. If any part of his plans seems to you inappropriate, please tell him and he will be glad to alter it." As he said this, Alan fixed the Jinnee with a stern eye.

The Jinnee's black eyes gleamed in response, but he bowed respectfully. "I am at your command, Colonel."

"Very good," said McMahon. "I take it, Mr. Dinsmuir, that you will wish to be present?"

Alan felt he had far rather be a thousand miles away, but Miss Dirdle had been unequivocal and Bea inflexible. "Yes, I should like to attend," he said, suppressing a sigh, "but on no account do I desire a public acknowledgment of my presence."

"Excellent," the colonel said smoothly. "Though naturally I cannot answer for His Highness's . . . ah . . . eagerness to show his appreciation, I shall advise him that you would prefer a private audience."

A private audience with the Prince Regent? All too easy to make some shocking mistake in etiquette! Though Alan wanted to turn tail and run, he did not dare demur. He managed to squeak out something which sounded like thanks.

"This is the Music Room, where the entertainment will take place," announced the colonel as they entered a huge chamber.

Alan stopped dead, dumfounded. The walls were painted with Chinese landscapes in gold on crimson, framed by gigantic *trompe l'oeil* serpents and winged, fire-breathing dragons. High above was an octagonal cornice, richly carved and gilded, and still higher, elliptical windows of coloured glass and then a tier patterned in blue and gold. Over all, a dome formed of gilded scallop shells rose to an elaborate center-piece from which hung a huge chandelier, with four gold dragons in flight below the glass lustre, presently unlit. There were several more chandeliers, only slightly less elaborate, their glass panels painted with Chinese figures.

Developing a crick in his neck, Alan lowered his gaze. Between the landscape panels stood porcelain pagodas some fifteen feet tall. The floor was covered with a vast blue carpet spangled with gold stars and fabulous oriental creatures. Even the furniture was all gilt, with mythical beasts holding up the arms.

Surely the Emperor of China himself could not boast more splendour! Alan began to fear even the Jinnee could not provide gifts to match such magnificence, not without falling into vulgar ostentation.

"Just between us," said Colonel McMahon, regarding him with sly amusement, "there are those who decry the place as mere vulgar ostentation, and shockingly extravagant besides. Of course, almost everything here is of English provenance. His Highness wishes to support our own manufactories. But on the other hand, he is always delighted to acquire genuine artifacts from the East, to be properly displayed in the more . . . ah . . . restrained apartments."

Alan seized his chance. "The cost to display, guard, and care for such valuables must be high," he said. "I shall be happy to help defray the expense."

The colonel nodded approvingly. "I shall so inform His Highness. No doubt his gratitude will increase commensurately."

With luck that meant no mere baronetcy, Alan hoped. Lord Hinksey would scarcely be impressed by anything less than a peerage. He *had* to win the marquis's favour. Bea, the darling girl, was quite willing to marry him without, but only a blackguard would let her cut herself off from her family for his sake.

Nothing must go wrong, and all depended on Col. Sir John McMahon, Private Secretary and Keeper of the Privy Purse. In accordance with Miss Dirdle's instructions, Alan said, "I should not wish you to be out of pocket, Colonel, in making arrangements for our spectacle. You must let me have an account of your expenses."

The colonel bowed.

"This apartment will be the perfect setting for what we have in mind," rumbled the Jinnee. "I am at your disposal, Colonel, to discuss the details."

McMahon took the Jinnee off to his office to consult, leaving Alan at liberty to wander through the public rooms, as the Prince was in his private apartments.

The Banqueting Room was even more extraordinary than the Music Room, with a huge silver dragon supporting the central chandelier. The other rooms, galleries, and passages were somewhat more modestly decorated, the Chinoiserie muted. Here, aesthetically refined gifts from the Jinnee might be better appreciated.

However, the whole left Alan uncomfortable. Unable to imagine actually living there, he wondered uneasily whether Bea would feel at home in these luxurious surroundings.

She was used to the sort of splendid mansions he had only viewed from the outside. For all he knew, the interior of Hinksey Hall was not so very different from the Royal Pavilion's drawing rooms and saloons. With the Jinnee's help, Alan could provide whatever she wanted, but he doubted he would ever be truly at ease with such unaccustomed grandeur.

Was her father right? Would she be happier in the end if she found a husband in her own world? Perhaps Alan was being selfish, and it would be the act of a blackguard to marry her even with the marquis's blessing.

# FIVE

When her beloved vanished from her arms, Bea went out with Miss Dirdle to the barouche, to return to Hinksey Hall.

"I wish I could have gone with him," Bea sighed as the carriage rolled through the village and turned down Headington Hill. "If I was at his elbow to give him the hint, there would be no chance of his making any *faux pas.*"

"Mr. Dinsmuir is far too intelligent to blunder," Miss Dirdle reassured her.

"Etiquette is so complicated, even if one is brought up to it. Suppose Alan somehow offends the Prince Regent, or Prinny simply fails to grant a patent of nobility? Without Papa's permission to wed, we should have to elope, and Alan refuses to contemplate such a drastic action."

"My dear Bea, you would be banished from Society for ever! Mr. Dinsmuir shows great good sense and a true gentlemanly instinct."

"Fustian! I should not mind, whereas without him I shall never be happy again," Bea said passionately.

She moped all the way home, but her megrims turned to dismay when she was met with a summons to her mother's sitting room. Could Mama have discovered that her frequent outings were not mere jaunts about the countryside, but calls at a certain cottage on the other side of town? As long as Miss Dirdle was with Bea, Lady Hinksey never enquired. Surely Reuben and Coachman would not betray her!

The marchioness's grave demeanor was not encouraging. "Sit down, Beatrice," she said. Bea sank into a chair. "I regret to tell you that I have been unable to persuade your father to permit you to accompany us to the Orfords' house party. In my opinion, an engagement contracted over the summer would go far to eliminate the disgrace of your earlier behaviour."

"An engagement, Mama?" Bea asked, startled. "To whom?"

Her mother waved a careless hand. "There are bound to be a number of eligible gentlemen staying with the Earl and Countess. However, Hinksey considers it best for you to remain in seclusion until the Little Season, when one may hope your misconduct will have been forgotten. He and I leave at the end of the week. I trust you will employ the fortnight of our absence in reflecting upon the reason for your papa's displeasure."

"Yes, Mama." Bea hoped she sounded sufficiently submissive, for her heart sang.

A whole fortnight! Tom must invite Alan to stay, she decided instantly.

Tom had returned from London just two days earlier, with Lord Wendover in tow. They spent the two days riding, shooting, fishing, and racing their curricles, seldom seen in the house except for meals. Bea had no chance to speak to them privately until the following evening, after dinner, when she ran them to earth in the billiard room.

"Want to play?" asked Tom. "M'cousin's a dab hand with a cue," he told his friend.

"Not now," said Bea. "I am sure Lord Wendover can give you a better game. You must enjoy having someone to keep you company."

"Yes, Windy's a great gun. I'll be sorry when he has to leave."

"Mother expects me at home by the end of the week," Lord Wendover explained sadly. "Otherwise, be happy to stay forever."

"You ought to invite someone else, Tom. Alan Dinsmuir, for instance."

"No, I say!" Tom exclaimed in alarm. "Dash it, Bea, I daresay the fellow don't even know how to sit a horse."

"Then you shall teach him," Bea proposed.

Tom's jaw dropped. *"Me?"*

"Who better? You are a capital goer, are you not?"

"I should say so," said Lord Wendover with enthusiasm. "Best seat of anyone I know."

"There you are, then. You drive to an inch, too, or so I have often heard you claim. It is a pity your shooting is less than accurate, but perhaps Alan will not mind."

"Dash it, Bea, there's nothing wrong with my aim, and I won't have you giving Dinsmuir the impression that there is!"

Bea clasped her hands in rapture. "Then you will teach him! You are the kindest cousin in the world, I vow."

"Dash it, Bea, I never said . . . Besides, my aunt and uncle won't like me inviting a stranger to stay."

"But he is not a stranger!" Bea said with wide-eyed innocence. "He is a fellow-student, a friend."

"Dash it, Bea, I've never even spoken to the fellow!"

"But Papa and Mama do not know that. They have no reason to suppose you have not been friends forever. Papa will raise no objection. He never has, since you came to live with us, though some of the boys you brought home from Eton were perfectly horrid!"

"But not one of 'em was a ramshackle, half-bred commoner," said Tom unwisely.

"Here, I say!" Lord Wendover expostulated. "Fellow she loves, remember."

Her emotions in tatters, Bea burst into tears, seized Tom's favourite cue from his hands, and took a wild swipe at him. Missing as he dodged, aghast, she snapped it in half on the table's edge and tossed the pieces among the balls. She swung round to march out, but Tom caught her arm.

"Dash it, Bea," he said shamefacedly, "I wasn't thinking. No harm in the fellow, I daresay. If he comes to stay while your parents are away, we can rub off any rough edges between us . . . Not saying there are any, mind!"

Bea flung her arms around his neck and wept into his cravat, to his acute discomfort. If this was what thwarted love did to his usually cheerful cousin, the sooner she married the fellow the better.

With his promise to speak to his uncle at once, Bea retired exhausted to her chamber. As she opened the door, something flickered in the corner of her eye. A moment later she was flying through the air.

"I thought you might like to see my pageant," said the Jinnee's voice in her ear.

"I would! It is to be tonight already?"

"The previously engaged singer has a sore throat."

"But what if someone recognizes me?"

"I cannot render you invisible, but I can deflect the glances of those about you, so that they never really notice you. Besides, all eyes will be on my fabulous spectacle!"

With that, Bea found herself standing next to Alan, at one end of a palatial, flamboyantly decorated room, brilliantly lit and very hot. In front of them, filling the near half of the chamber and facing the far end, were ranks of chairs occupied by chattering ladies and gentlemen in evening dress. Bea slipped her arm through Alan's, and he stared down at her in astonishment.

"I was just wishing you were here!" he said softly.

"Did you forget you have a Jinnee to grant your wishes?"

She smiled up at him. After a swift glance around, he bent his head to give her a brief kiss. At that moment, a triple knock came from the front of the room.

The Jinnee stood there, in his smoky robe and full trousers. Again he knocked thrice on the floor with a gold staff topped with a sinuous gold dragon. "My lords, ladies, and gentlemen, pray silence for the Sultan!"

Trumpets sounded. From one side entered a stout gentleman clad in a bejeweled tunic of gold and silver brocade over a floor-length crimson robe embroidered with gold thread. On his head he wore a curious headdress, so encrusted with gems that it flashed with every movement. Beneath this, the Prince Regent's plump face beamed at his stunned audience.

Alan groaned. "I never dreamt he meant to involve the Prince himself in the play-acting!" he whispered.

"His Royal Highness appears to be enjoying himself," Bea returned. "I have heard he often sings or plays the violoncello for his guests."

A storm of applause burst out as the spectators recovered their wits. With stately tread, Prinny advanced to a magnificent throne Bea had not observed amidst the general splendour. Seating himself, he held up his hands for silence, then clapped once, sharply.

Trumpets rang out again. The doors behind Alan and Bea opened, and in came a procession reminiscent of that which had caused such chaos in Oxford. They paraded down the aisle between the seats.

Bea was no expert, but to her eyes the forty maidens and forty Africans appeared to be dressed in an eclectic mixture of Arabian, Indian, and Chinese costumes, all richly embroidered. Half bore in their hands musical instruments: flutes and flageolets, lutes, harps and psalteries, tambourines, drums and cymbals. The rest carried objects on their heads, all different shapes and sizes, swathed in brilliant-hued cloths.

Reaching the open space between the audience and the Prince on his throne, the musicians divided to stand in a semicircle to either side. They began to play soft, solemn music with curious harmonies.

Between them, the rest came up one by one, knelt before the throne, placed their wrapped burdens on the floor, and salaamed. Then the music stopped. There was a breathless hush.

The Jinnee, now standing beside the throne, thumped with his rod. Once more the invisible trumpeters sounded a fanfare. The kneeling maidens and men whisked the cloths from their gifts, revealing the rarest of Chinese treasures. Porcelain bowls, vases, and statuettes; carvings in jade, onyx, and ivory; painted scrolls and fans: everything was exquisite, rare, and precious.

Gasping, the spectators leaned forward for a better

view, Prinny, too. Nothing could be better calculated to appeal to that acquisitive connoisseur.

Before the astonished whispers grew to a clamour, the Jinnee knocked again. The musicians started up a slow, sensuous tune, and the gift-bearers in the centre began to dance. Between the gifts they glided, weaving an ever-changing kaleidoscope of colour. The tempo gradually increased, and the pattern grew more and more complex. Soon the dancers were skipping around the fragile works of art.

In an agony of apprehension, Bea held her breath. She felt Alan's frozen tension at her side, and she knew that if she could tear her eyes from the dancers, she would see the entire audience immobile with disbelief.

Just when she must breathe or burst, the Jinnee's staff knocked once . . . twice . . . thrice. In the instant silence, all the candles went out.

Bea clutched Alan's arm. A woman screamed.

The Jinnee's voice rang through the room: "Behold, the Dragon."

A gleam of light appeared, high up in one corner, a silvery gleam. Scales glittered, as the monster circled the room with slow beats of great silver wings.

"It's the dragon from the banqueting room!" Alan breathed in Bea's ear. "Come to life . . ."

Spiraling inward, the dragon approached the huge chandelier hung from the centre of the dome. The smaller gold dragons beneath the lustre began to stir, then took wing. The carved dragons on the mantelpiece joined them, and even the *trompe l'oeil* dragons painted on the walls. All gleamed by their own light, a curious sight as they darted about the upper part of the room.

Scarlet flame flickered from the mouth of the great

silver dragon. One fiery breath lit every candle in the centre chandelier, while the smaller beasts ignited all the rest. As if banished by the flood of light, the silver giant vanished. Its brethren froze back in their accustomed places.

Bea blinked. Not only the dragon had vanished—dancers, musicians, and Jinnee were gone. The gifts now stood on an elegant but ordinary table before the throne—which was an ordinary (if ornate) armchair. Prinny stood behind the table, wearing the blue pelisse of the Light Dragoons, the Prince of Wales's Regiment. He looked distinctly self-satisfied.

At that moment, the room faded before Bea's eyes. She found herself flying through the air beneath the stars, which blurred into streaks as she sped faster and faster into the night.

Alan felt horribly alone and deserted when Bea disappeared. The audience pressed forward, at the Prince's invitation, to inspect his gifts. Moving against the tide, Colonel McMahon joined Alan.

"I never dreamt you were going to present such superb pieces," he said with a touch of incredulity, "and so many! They're worth a fortune."

"I acquired them at very little expense," Alan told him truthfully. A shilling and ninepence for an old copper lamp, to be precise. "There are more than I have space to display, and I can think of no one more likely to truly appreciate them than His Highness."

The colonel nudged him in the ribs. "Not to mention the little matter of a title," he said slyly. "I don't think there is going to be any trouble over that. His Highness is mightily pleased. Well, if you're sure you don't want to join the throng, I'll take you to his private library. He will be along shortly, I expect."

The library was far more to Alan's taste than the public rooms he had roamed the day before. The oriental influence was subdued, a patterned carpet in russet and dull blue, and aquamarine wallpaper with a white design. The furniture was elegant rather than eye-catching, the chandelier crystal without a dragon in sight. It depended from a ceiling painted to resemble a summer sky—just the colour of Bea's eyes—with puffs of white cloud, a fancy Alan rather liked.

He had time to glance at the books in the bookcases, and to note a novel by Miss Austen lying open upon a table. He was nervously twirling one of a pair of large globes when Prinny arrived.

Afterwards, Alan remembered little other than the Prince's gracious affability, but one moment stuck in his mind.

"Now do tell me, my dear fellow, how did you manage that business with the dragons? We have never seen such a realistic illusion. Spectacular!"

"I . . . I . . ." Alan stammered. "That is, I fear I don't know how it is done, sir. It is my secretary's secret. I leave that side of things to him."

Prinny laughed, his vast belly shaking, and winked at McMahon. "Nothing like having a master magician for a secretary, Mr. Dinsmuir! There are times we could do with one, eh, Sir John? Well, we thank you again for your notable contribution to our little place here. You will find us not ungenerous in remembering your generosity." He held out his hand.

Alan bowed low and backed out. Outside the door, he leant weakly against the wall, dabbing his brow. It had gone quite well, he thought. Prinny had not

seemed offended by what could be regarded as a refusal to explain the dragons, but had his laugh hidden
a royal chagrin?

Perhaps he would only grant a knighthood, or no
title at all. If so, Bea was lost to Alan forever. Why
the deuce had the Jinnee thrown in a horde of live
dragons?

McMahon came out. "Viscountcy," he said laconi-
cally. "Those dragons turned the trick. People will be
talking of them for weeks, and there is nothing he
likes better. I shall notify the Heralds' College and the
*London Gazette*. You will get your Patent of Nobility in
a week or two, by Royal Messenger. By the way, I don't
believe I have your direction?"

Alan's euphoria changed into panic. Wadham College? he wondered. Cherry Tree Cottage? "I shall be
traveling about a lot in the next fortnight," he said
hastily. "I'll send my secretary to pick up the patent.
Er, you did say viscount, didn't you?"

"That's right. It's quite proper to use the title immediately. Allow me to congratulate you, my lord."
He bowed with a sardonic air, only just not a sneer.

Let him sneer, Alan thought, striding jauntily towards the inn. McMahon had pocketed his bribe
quickly enough. It was not the first title sold for good
value; doubtless it would not be the last. For darling
Bea's sake . . .

Already walking on air, Alan scarcely noticed at first
when his steps started climbing into the sky. Then he
was rushing through the darkness, homeward he as-
sumed.

Homeward—what he needed now was a home fit
for a viscount, and more important, fit for a viscount's
bride.

# SIX

"A house?" said Mrs. Dinsmuir at the breakfast table. "Oh yes, dearest, we have thought of that, have we not, Mr. Jinnee?"

The Jinnee beamed. "Yes, indeed, my lord. Miss Dirdle—admirable woman!—suggested weeks past that you would require a suitable dwelling."

"We did not want to add another burden when you had so much else to worry over, so we talked about it when you and dear Bea were walking in the garden. We have everything in train."

Alan half-choked on a piece of sausage. The Jinnee thumped him on the back.

Recovering, he asked in dismay, "Mother, you haven't gone and bought a house, have you? Bea must be consulted, and I should like *some* say in the choice."

"Of course, dear. Besides, you will want a new house, not someone else's old one, with the neighbours regarding you as intruders and constantly making comparisons with the last residents."

"New! Bea and I can't wait while a new house is built."

"A night's work," said the Jinnee with a sort of modest benevolence.

"Good Lord, this isn't ancient China! If a house

mushrooms overnight, it won't be simply a nine days'
wonder, like Aladdin's. I dare not even contemplate
the legal repercussions!"

"We may not be lawyers, Alan," his mother said
sharply, "but we have not all lost our wits. Mr. Jinnee
has kindly combed the country for land for sale. He
has found several parcels where a building may be
erected out of sight of all neighbours and roads. People may wonder why they saw no signs of construction,
but they cannot be sure it did not take place in the
normal way."

The Jinnee gave her a nod of approval. "I put down
earnest money on all the plots," he told Alan. "I shall
take you and Lady Beatrice to inspect them and make
your choice. You have only to give the word."

"You're waiting for me to give the word?" Alan said
a trifle sourly. "That makes a change!"

Mrs. Dinsmuir took him severely to task for ingrati-
tude. The Jinnee—his servant!—had not the grace to
make himself scarce, but listened with a bland smile
to the scolding. Alan was rescued by a knock on the
door, heralding the arrival of Bea and Miss Dirdle.

Bea rushed into his arms. "Alan darling, did it
work?"

She did not seem to mind that he was too busy kissing her to answer. Mrs. Dinsmuir took it upon herself
to enlighten Miss Dirdle. "My son is made viscount!"
she announced proudly.

Drawing back, Bea cried, "A viscount? Oh, Alan,
how simply splendid. Papa cannot possibly object to
a viscount." She ran to the Jinnee and kissed his cheek.
"It is all due to your magnificent spectacle, Mr. Jinnee.
How can we ever thank you?"

The Jinnee kissed her back, with more enthusiasm

than Alan considered proper. He frowned. Suppose the Jinnee fell in love with Bea? It was practically inevitable, irresistible as she was.

In the old tale, a wicked magician had stolen Aladdin's wife and palace. What if the Jinnee decided to emulate his example? As soon as his three months' service was up, he could fly away with her to anywhere in the world—or out of it.

If only Alan had never mentioned Lord Mansfield's ruling on slavery, the Jinnee would still be bound to the lamp and forced to obey its owner. Now the lamp stood useless on the mantel shelf, while the insubordinate Jinnee no longer waited for orders before acting as he saw fit.

At least he still had to obey direct orders, for the next two months. All Alan could do was ensure he and Bea were wed by then, make his last command a prohibition against parting them, and hope everything would not vanish the instant the Jinnee was free. Including Bea.


Bea sensed Alan's uneasiness. Though he was now Viscount Dinsmuir, he still seemed to doubt a happy ending to their love. The best way to cheer him was to marry him as soon as possible, and she was nothing loath.

The Jinnee flew them, along with Mrs. Dinsmuir and Miss Dirdle, all over the country to choose a place to live. Not surprisingly, the most safely secluded tracts of land were in the outer reaches, the Lake District, Northumberland, the Welsh mountains, even the Scottish Highlands. Most were beautiful, but not at all what Bea had in mind.

"We need somewhere within reach of London," she said. "Alan is going to be an important member of the House of Lords. There are few with legal training! Besides, I should like Papa and Mama to see our house before we marry, just to reassure them, so it must not be too far from Oxford. I refuse to wait until they can travel to Scotland!"

"I believe I have the very thing," said the Jinnee, grinning. "I didn't take you there first in case his lord-ship suspected me of trying to influence you."

Shortly they stood on a south-facing hillside in the Cotswolds, looking down into a wooded valley. Clumps of harebells dotted the short turf. No house was visible, no cottage or shepherd's hut, no chimney pot, not even a plume of smoke. The only sounds were the distant bleating of sheep, and a lark trilling its heart out overhead.

Bea gripped Alan's hand tighter. "Do you like it?"

He looked down at her. "If you do."

"It is perfect! We shall call it Lark Hill."

"The contract is ready to be signed, my lord," the Jinnee said, now playing the businesslike secretary. "If you do that tomorrow, I shall build your house the following night."

"Then a carriage road must be constructed to the nearest public lane," said the practical Miss Dirdle. "Flying is all very well in its way—indeed, most enjoy-able—but a more generally accepted method of in-gress and egress is required."

"And you must choose your furnishings, Bea dear," put in Mrs. Dinsmuir. "It is no good leaving that to the gentlemen."

"First you must choose the kind of house, Bea,"

Alan said. "Do you want a grand mansion like your father's?"

"Heavens no! But it must be large enough to hold political house parties when you have made your name in Parliament. And nursery space for plenty of children, too."

Alan blushed. "You hear her, Jinnee?" he said hurriedly.

"I hear and obey, my lord."

*"Don't* stud the windows with emeralds and rubies, like Aladdin's. Or any other precious stones! Ordinary wood and glass will do. Nor do we want the house built of jasper, carnelian, and alabaster."

"Might I suggest Cotswold stone?" Miss Dirdle proposed.

"Yes, Cotswold stone," Bea agreed. "It is a very pretty colour, and it should please our neighbours."

Recalling the Jinnee's admiration of Prinny's Brighton retreat, Alan said firmly, "Not a copy of the Royal Pavilion."

"No," said Bea, wrinkling her nose, "but I believe His Highness has all the latest in plumbing and steam heating, and kitchen contrivances. Can you provide those, Jinnee?"

"Certainly, my lady. I shall study the subject tonight."

"Darling, how practical you are," said Alan adoringly.

Bea kissed him, and the world whirled about her—not that his kisses did not always make her head whirl, but this time the Jinnee chose the moment to take them back to Cherry Tree Cottage.

\* \* \*

Next day the papers were signed; Lark Hill became the property of Viscount Dinsmuir. At sunset, the Jinnee vanished to set about constructing the house.

In the morning, when Alan came down from his tiny chamber under the eaves, the Jinnee was sitting at the breakfast table, digging into a vast plateful of ham and eggs—he had adopted English notions of breakfast with delight. He looked exceedingly pleased with himself.

"Sausages and muffins, my lord?" he enquired.

"No, what you're having smells good. I'll have the same, please, but not quite as much!"

The Jinnee shimmered momentarily. A maidservant popped into existence, properly dressed in grey with white cap and apron. Setting down on the table a tray with a covered plate, rack of toast, and pot of coffee, she disappeared again.

"Well?" asked Alan, sitting down.

"Very well! The house is ready for painting, papering, and furnishing, unless her ladyship desires to make any alterations. It is built of Cotswold stone—an attractive material, I may say—and not at all in the style of the Royal Pavilion."

"No jewels around the windows?"

"None, my lord. Nor the least trace of alabaster, carnelian, or jasper, though I did venture to use some marble, having observed that stone at Hinksey Hall.

"Excellent! We'll go and see it as soon as Bea and Miss Dirdle arrive."

Bea had to wait to see her parents off for their house party before she and Miss Dirdle could set out for Headington.

"Bring Dinsmuir back with you," demanded Tom,

eager for male company after Lord Wendover's departure.

"I shall," Bea promised, as he handed her into the barouche, "and his mother, too. It turns out she and Miss Dirdle have been acquainted this age." Several weeks, at any rate.

"Another ex-governess, is she? Pretty good to find herself the mother of a viscount! Never fear, Bea, I'll do my best to teach the fellow what he needs to do you credit."

Bea bit her lip. It was no good pointing out Alan's manifest superiority in everything but riding, driving, and shooting, since those were all that counted with her insouciant cousin.

Alan awaited her arrival with his usual impatience, but the Jinnee was even more impatient to display his handiwork. He allowed scarce a moment for greetings before he whisked them all off to Lark Hill. They landed on a leveled space before the—*house?* Bea gasped and Alan groaned. A *pagoda?*

No, not quite, for the building was not tall and narrow, like the pagoda in the Queen's Gardens at Kew. A Chinese palace, perhaps. Unmistakably Chinese, with the turned-up corners of the curved roofs, like the points of a tricorn hat. Roofs plural; the four storeys, each smaller than the one below, were clearly marked by lines of roofing protecting pillared verandahs.

"It is beautiful," said Mrs. Dinsmuir stoutly.

"Yes, it is," Bea admitted, "but I fear it will not do."

"Not do?" thundered the Jinnee, and he grew by several inches in all directions. "I observed your every stricture! It is like neither Hinksey Hall nor the Brighton Pavilion. I used local materials, save the mar-

ble pillars. No gems or semiprecious stones, not even
a mosaic or a single painted tile! Why, I—"

"Calm yourself, Mr. Jinnee!" cried Mrs. Dinsmuir.
She laid a hand on his agitated arm, and he promptly
shrank to his usual size. "I am very much afraid dear
Bea is right. You see, Alan's rise to his present position
has been decidedly unconventional, so anything
which draws attention to its oddity must be avoided."

"Like the plague," growled Alan.

"Also," put in Miss Dirdle, "anyone might suppose
they had simply not noticed a perfectly ordinary house
in this spot, but no one could overlook the sudden
appearance of so impressive and unusual an edifice."

The Jinnee sighed, and trees bent before the gale
of his breath. "If you say so, ladies. But I put my heart
into it."

"I am so sorry." Bea squeezed his hand. "It is perfectly splendid. Perhaps later . . . a summer house,
Alan?"

"An excellent notion," Alan said, with what struck
Bea as a false heartiness. "Jinnee, can you rebuild tonight, in the local style as well as the local stone?"

"Yes, my lord," said the Jinnee mournfully, and vanished. An instant later the Chinese palace vanished,
too, along with every last sign of its existence save the
leveled space on the hillside.

Still sad, the Jinnee reappeared and took them
home to the cottage, whence they repaired by normal
means to Hinksey Hall.


That afternoon, Bea had to force herself not to
hover anxiously over Alan's first riding lesson. She
spent the time showing Mrs. Dinsmuir around Hink-

sey Hall and discussing the decoration and furniture
she wanted in her own new home. The Jinnee accompanied them, taking careful note of her every word.
No more disastrous misunderstandings!

On the morrow, with Alan appropriated by Tom,
the ladies went to see the Jinnee's second effort. They
all warmly applauded the charming manor house. Bea
had one request:

"Would you mind *weathering* it a bit? Just so that it
looks fifty or a hundred years old, but very well kept
up, of course."

"Done!" He waved his hand. The edges of stones
blurred and softened, and patches of lichen appeared
on the roof.

The decorating and furnishing took several days;
then the Jinnee planted gardens and kitchen gardens
to order. Next, Mrs. Dinsmuir and Miss Dirdle set
about hiring servants, while the Jinnee filled the coach
house with carriages and the stables with riding and
carriage horses. By then, Alan had ceased to stagger
around stiff-legged as a stork after each riding lesson.
He even foresaw the prospect of one day enjoying being on horseback. Tom was pleased with his driving,
too, though partly because he was confident Alan
would never surpass his own skill.

Two weeks had sped by. The Hinkseys came home.

Bea wanted Alan to let her parents get to know
him before he approached her father to ask for her
hand. She was as eager as he to be married, but she
saw no real need for haste. Alan did not explain his
fears about what the Jinnee would do once his quarter's service was finished. The morning after the
Hinkseys' return, he begged a private interview with
the marquis.

Lord Hinksey raised his eyebrows in surprise, but silently led the way to the library, a large room walled with unread books collected by generations of noble ancestors. "This is very sudden!" he said, waving Alan to a chair.

"Not really, sir. I was acquainted with Lady Beatrice before Tom invited me to stay. In this past fortnight, a slight acquaintance has blossomed into . . . something warmer. I wish to request your permission to make her my wife."

"Hmph! And she is not averse to your suit?"

"So she has given me to understand, sir."

"You had best believe it then. My girl ain't slow to say no! Lord Dinsmore . . . a viscountcy, eh? Well, it's not a dukedom," muttered Lord Hinksey, "but it seems that wretched fellow has already got himself betrothed to some other female!" Aloud, he said, "Don't believe I ever knew your father."

"He died young, sir," Alan said cautiously.

"Ah, before he inherited the title, of course, hence your mother's lack . . . Not that I mean to cavil at that, my boy! Charming lady, Mrs. Dinsmuir. I daresay you are able to support Bea in the proper style, ha ha?"

"Certainly, sir. I have a house at Lark Hill, near Ascott under Wychwood, which Bea has seen and approves." As she should, having helped to plan it. "And I have a large income from the Funds. My secretary will be pleased to give you the details . . ."

"Gad no!" said the marquis in horror. Apparently Miss Dirdle was right again when she advised against Alan proffering too exact a knowledge of his own wealth. "Leave settlements and such to the lawyers! Well, well. I'll have a word with Bea's mama, but she'll be only too pleased. Several ladies at the Orfords' dared to doubt that . . . Well, no matter. This will put such talk to rest. I'll send a notice to the *Morning Post* at once!"

For Bea, the last month before her wedding raced by. She knew Alan was fretting.

He wanted to send the Jinnee to purchase a special license, so as to marry her immediately. He did not understand the need for a trousseau, when the Jinnee could instantly provide all she desired. Nor did he appreciate the propriety of having the banns read in Christ Church Cathedral in Oxford, especially after such a brief courtship and betrothal.

At last the day came, a bright, warm Saturday morning in August. Entering the cool dimness of the cathedral, Bea was scarcely conscious of her father's sleeve beneath her fingertips, nor of the tenants and servants in the back pews and the dukes, duchesses, marquises and marchionesses, earls and countesses in the front. She saw, but her mind did not register, the grinning groomsman—Cousin Tom. All her awareness was on the tall, lean figure at his side.

Tall, lean, and elegant, in his perfectly fitted blue morning coat and buff Inexpressibles. Memory took her back to the Cherwell, that morning just three months past, when a poor, shabby scholar had rescued an elderly gentlewoman from drowning. He was titled now, and wealthy, but he was still the same gentle, unassuming man she had fallen in love with on the spot.

And as she approached, their eyes met with the same shock of recognition, the instant affinity which had made her decide that same day that she was going to marry him.

Alan's eyes met Bea's, and nothing else had any importance. He touched her hand, and all his worries fell to ashes as a flame of tenderness and desire scorched through his veins. His heart soared to the vaulted roof and fluttered there, singing like a skylark.

Throughout the service, he saw only her face. The walk back down the aisle, the drive to Hinksey Hall, the wedding breakfast, all passed in a haze.

Then they were in the carriage taking them to Lark Hill, alone together at last, and all that mattered was the warm, responsive body in his arms, the soft, sweet lips meeting his. The world whirled about them, but neither spared a thought for the Jinnee.

Not until morning. Waking, Alan recalled his fears. How could he have forgotten to forbid the Jinnee to part him from his wife, his love, his life? Bea was at his side, still asleep, locked in his embrace—but the Jinnee was now free.

She might vanish at any moment.

He held her close, made passionate love to her when she awoke, refused to let her leave his sight.

It was near noon when they left their chamber and went down to break their fast. Their new butler bowed them into the breakfast room. At the table sat Miss Dirdle, Mrs. Dinsmuir, and the Jinnee.

The two ladies rushed to embrace the blushing bride. The Jinnee heaved himself to his feet and came over to Alan, to shake his hand and slap him on the back.

"Sorry to interrupt the idyll, my boy," he said heartily, "but your mama and I have news we didn't want to keep from you any longer. I trust you have no objection to a Jinnee for a stepfather?"

# EPILOGUE

Mr. and Mrs. Jinnee settled in a *cottage orné à la chinoise* on the grounds of Lark Hill, where they lived happily together for many years. In pride of place on their drawing room mantel shelf stood a brightly polished copper lamp.

The Jinnee was a great favourite with his stepgrandchildren, of whom he had many (educated, of course, by Miss Dirdle, still hale and romantic at heart at eighty-five). Grandpapa Jinnee, after all, could be relied upon to supply quite the most marvelous birthday presents imaginable!

# THE SEVEN RAVENS

by
**Karla Hocker**

# ONE

"*Seven* brothers?!" Incredulous, Lady Emily Marchmont stared at the white-haired solicitor, ensconced
behind her late father's desk.

"Seven," Mr. Wordsworth repeated solemnly.

"I am *not* an only child?"

"You are the only issue of his lordship's second marriage. The sons are the issue of the first marriage."

Lady Emily rose. She needed movement, air. In a
few brisk strides she crossed the faded Turkey rug in
the spacious study and flung open a set of French
doors leading onto the east terrace of her home, Briar
Cottage. The April breeze was cool and bracing, and
she stood for a moment, welcoming the blustering
wind in hopes that it might clear her mind.

Seven brothers. And she never knew.

"I didn't think I'd live to see the day when you're
speechless, Lady Emily."

She spun. Mr. Wordsworth's smile was kind, pater-
nal, more so than her father's had ever been. Actually,
she couldn't remember her father smiling.

"I don't quite know what to say." Lady Emily started
to pace, a black-slippered foot kicking the hem of her
mourning gown with every energetic step. "Here I
am, twenty-two years old, and my father had to die

before I learned that he had sons. That I had brothers. Seven of them! I ask you, what kind of man would keep that secret from his daughter?"

Mr. Wordsworth watched her for a moment. She was tall, slender, with the dark hair and eyes of a true Marchmont and no resemblance at all to her mother, who had once been toasted as the Golden Venus. He could have told Lady Emily that it was a bitter, disillusioned man who kept such secrets. But he didn't.

He said, "I suggested more than once that you should be told, but his lordship was adamant. He did not want you to know until he was in his grave. And although, no doubt, he meant for you to hear this during the reading of the will, he did not specify so, and I felt at liberty to have this little talk with you before Mr. Marchmont comes in."

"Cousin Harold!" Lady Emily stopped in her tracks. "Does he know? Lud! What a dust-up there'll be. He won't inherit the title, and he has forever fancied himself the Earl of Shoffield."

"Mr. Marchmont does know, but he believes your brothers dead. And now, Lady Emily, much as it may go against the grain with you, pray sit down and say nothing until I've told you what little I know of the affair."

Lady Emily returned to her chair in front of the desk. Hands folded demurely in her lap, she said, "My lips are buttoned and I won't fidget. And that's a promise. Only, please tell it quickly, Mr. Wordsworth."

His mouth twitched a little, but he did as bidden. "Your father had been widowed two years when he met your mother and married her out of hand. He was one-and-sixty, and she was no older than you are now. Two-and-twenty. That, as I understand it, was what started the rift between your father and his sons, the eldest being thirty, and the youngest thirteen or thereabouts."

Emily closed her mouth firmly. She had promised not to interrupt, and she wouldn't. She had no recollection of her mother and not the slightest notion why she had married a man thrice her age, but it seemed the silliest thing that her father's sons—her brothers—had taken exception to a young stepmother.

"When you were about two years old," Mr. Wordsworth said, "there was, apparently, an especially violent disagreement between your father and Edward, the eldest son. I don't know what it was about, but your brothers left that same day and never returned."

Emily clutched the arms of her chair to stop herself from jumping up and pacing. Two years old! Then she must know her brothers. She must have seen them. Surely she should have *some* tiny bit of memory of seven young men?

"You lived at Shoffield Court then. Do you remember that, Lady Emily?"

"Yes, of course. It is a horrid old place. Dark and cold. But I don't remember my brothers. Or even my mother. Which is strange, is it not? We left there after Mama's death, and I was two then, so Father and I must have left shortly after my brothers did. Why can I remember a house, but not a mother or brothers?"

"You lived at Shoffield Court another two years, Lady Emily. Until you were four and a half. Then your father brought you here because he feared at Shoffield Court you'd hear gossip about the family as you grew older."

She frowned in confusion. "I believed it was right

after my mother's death when—but never mind. Do you know where my brothers are now?"

Before Mr. Wordsworth could reply, a dry cough announced the presence of Mr. Harold Marchmont. Emily fought down irritation. Cousin Harold was the son of her father's second cousin. The heir presumptive. By no means was he a frequent visitor at Briar Cottage, but he never knocked, always sneaked into a room, and one never knew how long he'd been listening.

"Your brothers, my dear Emily," Cousin Harold said in the dulcet, patronizing tone she disliked, "are dead."

She scowled at him as he inserted his portly bulk into the chair beside her. He was ten years older than she, and almost always, when he opened his mouth, he was correct in every dratted utterance he made.

"But your mother did not die," Harold Marchmont continued complacently. "At least, not twenty years ago, though she may be dead now. But back then, she cuckolded your father. Ran off with a lover."

Emily was unaware of rising and slapping him—until she felt the sting in her palm and saw the red marks on Harold's cheek.

"Tut, tut, my dear." The solicitor's voice was soothing rather than reproachful.

"Beg your pardon, Mr. Wordsworth. I'll sit down again." Emily suited action to the words. "But I won't apologize to Cousin Harold."

"I said nothing that isn't true." Harold pressed a crisp, snowy handkerchief against his smarting face. "However, I'm not surprised at your behavior. You've always had a wild, ungoverned streak."

"We can discuss my behavior—and yours—later,"

Emily said with icy politeness. "Kindly let Mr. Wordsworth speak now. Anything I should know about my mother and brothers, I would like to hear from him, not from you."

Mr. Wordsworth said, "Unfortunately, there isn't much more I can tell you, Lady Emily. When your father first engaged my services, you and his lordship had been living here a little over a year. He was still quite vigorous then and frequently traveled to Shoffield Court. However, he'd suffered a nasty fall, which put him in mind to write a new will, and sending for his York solicitor would have taken several days.'

"Patience was not Father's strong suit," said Emily.

"Nor is it yours," muttered Harold.

Emily ignored him. "What about my mother, Mr. Wordsworth?"

"I was given to understand that your mother left Shoffield Court when you were two. That's all. Lord Shoffield made it clear he did not wish to pursue the topic further."

"She left," Emily repeated. She did not look at Harold. There was no need; she *knew* his pink, round face would have the smooth, satisfied look of a man once again proven correct. Emily leaned toward the solicitor. "Are you saying I may have a mother as well as brothers?"

Mr. Wordsworth looked unhappy. "I do not know, Lady Emily. I do not know whether your mother is alive or dead. And neither do I know with certainty that your brothers are alive."

"They're dead," said Cousin Harold. "They joined Sir Lawrence Raven's men and were guillotined in Paris."

Emily's stomach twisted, but she couldn't be certain

whether it was the image of the guillotine or the name Raven that affected her more strongly.

Mr. Wordsworth said, "Now that you're here, Mr. Marchmont, there's no point delaying the reading of the will. There is a codicil, added only last month, that may shed some light on the question of Lady Emily's mother and brothers."

When the solicitor finished reading, a thick silence hung in the air. The will made no mention of Emily's mother. The codicil, however, did pertain to her brothers. Her father had, indeed, received a report of their deaths in France, but he had strong reason to believe the report was false. He wanted his daughter to find the truth. And to that purpose, she must go to Ravenhill.

Ravenhill! Emily's heart raced. Was there no end to surprises this day? Mother, brothers, she would embrace happily if fate so decreed. But, go to Ravenhill?

Impossible.

"Lady Emily?" Mr. Wordsworth had stepped around the desk and was patting her shoulder. "This is encouraging news, is it not? Your father, apparently, had reason to believe that the key to your brothers' whereabouts lies at Ravenhill. I understand it's situated not too far from here. I shall be glad to accompany you before I leave."

"I cannot go!" She had come close to shouting at the elderly man and rose hastily to walk off the agitation that threatened to suffocate her.

The solicitor watched her with a searching, puzzled look. "Do you not wish to find the truth, Lady Emily? If your brothers are alive, surely they have a right to their inheritance."

"They're dead," said Cousin Harold. "And I shall

start proceedings immediately to have them legally declared dead and buried."

"Which is precisely why Father asked *me* to look into the matter." Emily all but tore the hem of her gown as she strode up and down the study. "He knew you wouldn't pursue anything detrimental to your own interests."

"Why then do you hesitate to fulfill your father's wish, Lady Emily?" asked Mr. Wordsworth.

She cast him an anguished look.

"Because," Cousin Harold said smoothly, "our dear Emily compromised herself at Ravenhill."

She had indeed compromised herself. Quite thoroughly. And now she was on her way to see the man who had humiliated her.

Emily stared out the carriage window. Ordinarily, she would have ridden, but there was nothing ordinary about this visit to Ravenhill, which she had last seen six years ago. She needed every shred of self-confidence, and even though a two-hour ride would have lifted her spirits, the boost would not have sufficed to carry her through that first moment of seeing Alex again, not if she was heated and disheveled and smelled like a stable lad. No, she needed to know that she looked her best. That her shoes and gown were dust free. That every curl was in place. That her heart and pulse beat slow and steady—if only they would!

The morning was balmy, but gray and humid. Now and again, a spatter of rain hit the coach, and Emily could only pray that the weather held, or they'd be mired on this marshy stretch of road on the way home. She had been warned, of course. But after a night of soul-searching and a painfully wrung decision in the early morning hours, she would not, for any reason, postpone this visit lest she never make it at all.

Drat! Her hands were shaking. She should have ridden after all. Any ordeal diminished in severity when she raced across the land. But then Cousin Harold would have insisted on accompanying her and would have had total support from Fletcher, the head groom, who drew the line when it came to her crossing Romney Marsh by herself. He'd have stoically held on to her reins until Harold was mounted. As it was, she must be grateful that Fletcher hadn't mentioned Lady Raven's absence to anyone but her.

Emily glanced at the woman seated beside her—knitting, despite the frequent jolts and bounces. Mary, her maid, who had been the nursery maid and, together with Miss Reeling, the governess, had once comprised all the "family" Emily knew. She had scarcely seen her father until she turned fourteen, when he announced that they must get better acquainted and she should join him at dinner every night and for a game of chess or cards afterward. That year, her father also started to invite Cousin Harold and his widowed mother to spend a few weeks at Briar Cottage every summer.

"Mary, did you come from Shoffield Court?"

"No, deary." The woman, whose tightly pulled brown hair showed the first strands of gray, rested the knitting in her lap and met Emily's searching look. "None of the staff at Briar Cottage came from Shoffield Court."

"But . . . you did know about my brothers? And my mother? Before last night, I mean. Before Mr. Wordsworth spoke to you."

"I wouldn't say I knew, Lady Emily. There was a flurry of rumors some years back, but his lordship made no bones about it that anyone caught gossiping would be dismissed. I thought no more about it, but it all came back last night when Mr. Wordsworth spoke to us in the servants hall. And we're all ever so pleased that you'll have Briar Cottage, Lady Emily, no matter what."

Yes, Emily would have her home. And an income to see her very comfortably settled for life.

Or she would have a fortune. If her brothers weren't found. If Cousin Harold succeeded in having them declared dead. Because her father's will provided, if Harold should inherit title and estate, then *all* income from funds and investments not falling under the provisions of the entail would come to her.

"What were the rumors, Mary?"

The maid looked uncomfortable. "Something about Lady Shoffield, I think. I don't quite recollect, Lady Emily."

"You just said it all came back to you last night."

"Is that thunder I hear?" Mary peered out the window. "Lightning bolts, too. Fletcher was right. 'Tis not a good day to be traveling."

"Don't digress, Mary. I want to hear about the rumors."

The older woman's mouth tightened in a way Emily recognized all too well.

"Don't be stubborn, Mary," she said softly. "Surely I've been kept in the dark long enough. Father is gone and cannot give me the truth. There's no harm in your telling me whatever you've heard."

Mary looked at her through narrowed eyes. She sighed. "I warrant you're right, deary. But considering that the gossip came from Mrs. Marchmont's abigail, you'd best take it with a grain of salt. They had just come from London and stopped for the night. And we thought it was strange that Mr. Harold wasn't with his mother. But Severn, Mrs. Marchmont's woman, said Mr. Harold wasn't one that could mind his tongue, and Mrs. Marchmont didn't want him along since nothing was settled nor confirmed."

"What needed confirmation?" Emily prompted when Mary fell silent and sat frowning at the half-finished muffler in her lap.

"Mrs. Marchmont heard talk of a woman that died in debtor's prison. A woman, rumored to be Lady Shoffield. And Severn told us that Mrs. Marchmont was set on informing his lordship, and that it was a just end for Lady Shoffield, after running off all those years ago with her husband's own son."

Emily sat stunned. "I don't believe it!"

"And who says you should? It's rumor, Lady Emily. Spiteful gossip. And the only reason I told you is that now, when his lordship won't be stopping you any longer from going to London for the season, you may be hearing more rubbish like that. You'll be a new face in town, and that always gives rise to gossip. So you'd best be prepared."

Again, Emily stared out the carriage window. It hadn't been her father's decree alone that kept her from London. True, while he was alive he would not have countenanced a stay in town, during the season or any other time, but that restriction had not bothered her. On the contrary. She wouldn't have gone to London for anything. Not after her foolishness at Ravenhill, because Alex Raven was known to stay in London quite frequently.

She noticed suddenly that they were on Raven land, and must have been for some time. It was land crisscrossed by drainage ditches and dikes carefully planned by Sir Lawrence Raven, father of Alexander.

Sir Alexander now.

Alex.

She could not breathe. She felt dizzy, her insides churned, and for a moment she feared she'd have to stop the carriage. A pungent odor bit her nostrils. She gasped, coughed, her eyes watering.

"Better?" asked Mary, calmly stoppering a bottle of smelling salts and returning it to the capacious bag at her side.

"You all but suffocate me with those noxious salts and ask if I'm better? Lud, Mary!" Emily smiled weakly. "You're a heartless wretch."

"You *are* better," Mary said with satisfaction. "And not a moment too soon. We're about to turn in the gates, and that's no time to be swooning or casting up your accounts."

Emily sat quite still. If she did not look out the window, if she did not let the sight of the Ravenhill lawns and gardens resurrect deeply buried memories, then she would be all right. At least long enough to step inside the house.

"Mary," she said suddenly. "Do you know my brothers' names? The eldest is Edward. But I quite forgot to ask about the others."

"Can't help you there, Lady Emily. It proves, though, don't it, that I was right when I said no good will come of sudden starts. But you were ever this way. Made up your mind, and off you went with never a thought to consequences."

Yes, indeed, Mary was right. Not for the first time in her long years of service to Lady Emily Marchmont.

The carriage stopped and, lest she be overtaken by cowardice, Emily thrust the door open and leaped out before Fletcher could climb off his perch and let down the steps. Thunder rumbled close by. A gust of wind caught her pelisse, whipping it around her legs.

She hurried up a flight of marble steps to Ravenhill's impressive main entrance, and as she approached the front door, a desperate wish that Alex was in London, or in Canterbury with his mother and married sister, warred with determination to get the information she sought.

Emily clasped the bell pull, tugged sharply. If the bell pealed somewhere inside the vast old house, she did not hear it. A violent clap of thunder obliterated any other sound.

One wing of the heavy, carved door swung wide. And there, an open book in one hand, a distracted look on his face, stood Alexander Raven. More mature, perhaps a little wider in the shoulders, a little leaner in the face; but the same unruly burnished-brown hair, the same hazel eyes. The same Alex.

And Emily felt the same longing that had devoured her six years ago, the all but impossible to resist craving that had driven her into his arms.

Into his bed.

# TWO

Incapable of speech, Emily gazed up at Alex. And he did not even seem to recognize her, merely gave her a preoccupied frown before looking at the book in his hand and closing it.

From the corner of her eye, she caught a flash of lightning, accompanied by a thunderclap so powerful it shook the ground. Some unseen force knocked against her back, propelling her headlong into the entry, and she would have fallen if Alex had not caught her in his arms. She heard cracking, splintering sounds, the stomping and whinnying of horses, Mary's scream . . . and Alex's voice.

"Emily, are you all right?" His hands held her steady. His eyes, dark with concern, searched her face. "Can you hear me? Can you speak?"

She wasn't sure. That brief moment when he had held her in his arms, and now the feel of his hands on her shoulders, plain took her breath away and made her tremble all over.

Finally, she managed to ask, "What happened?"

"Lightning struck the pillar behind you."

She smelled the charred wood even before she turned and saw the blackened remains of a once tall, intricately carved pillar and the ragged, smoldering edge of the portico.

Lightning flashed again. Thunder crashed. Stable boys came running with blankets and shovels, footmen and maids with buckets of water. They milled around the front steps, but none of their fire-fighting equipment was needed since the earlier, occasional spatter of rain was now a deluge, whipped by a fierce wind. One of the men shouted a brief command, and everyone took off at a run toward the kitchen entrance.

Emily did not see her carriage. "Mary!" she cried anxiously. "Alex—my maid! Where is she? And Fletcher. Did the horses bolt?"

"They did not," Alex assured her. "Your groom had trouble holding them and drove on. No doubt, he took your maid around to the back."

He drew her farther into the entrance hall and shut the door. He looked at her, and the vast hall seemed to shrink to a mere three-foot circle, enclosing her and Alex. A circle from which she had neither the strength nor the will to escape.

His smile teased. "Such a tempestuous entrance, and now, not a word or a move. This is unlike you, Emily. Or have you changed so very much over the years?"

"You might say I was struck dumb," she murmured, intent on studying every plane and angle of his lean face. "It won't last, Alex."

"I daresay you're right. In fact, I feel stricken myself. If you hadn't quite literally blown into my arms, I don't know how I would have—but I am rambling. What you need is a glass of wine. You're still shaking."

And so she was. From the shock of a lightning strike close to her? Or from the shock of finding herself as moonstruck by the mere sight of him as she had been as a sixteen-year-old?

She saw Alex watching her quizzically.

"Thank you," she managed. "Wine would be welcome." Without conscious thought she turned toward the front room, where, one day, long ago, they had played chess for ten blissful hours. Her toe sent something skittering on the marble floor. "I'm sorry! Your book. You must have dropped it."

"All in the service of chivalry." He pocketed the slender volume, then placed an arm around her shoulders, propelling her firmly into the sitting room and into a chair.

Still trembling—and this time she was certain it was caused by his touch—she accepted the glass he handed her, quaffed the contents in a most unladylike manner. The liquid burned all the way down her throat, into her stomach.

"Lud!" Eyes watering, she gasped for air. "That wasn't wine."

"Brandy." His voice betrayed amusement. "It's supposed to be sipped. As, if I may point out, is wine."

"Not when you're shaking like a leaf because you must face the man who once made a complete fool of you."

"Now, there's the Emily I knew. Plainspoken and to the point." He nodded approvingly, face solemn, but not bothering to hide the laughter in his eyes. "Even if, as usual, she is wide off the mark. *I* was the fool in that long ago past. What was it—six years?"

"Alex, don't you dare laugh!" Indignation went a long way to help restore her composure. "What you did to me was bad enough, and I had sworn never to see you again. And I wouldn't have, but for Father's will."

She saw his gaze move over the black skirts showing under her pelisse. An emerald pelisse. Even though she would wear mourning for a cold and distant father, she had not deemed it necessary to order black out-door wear since she hardly ever made formal visits.

"You did not know my father died?"

"No. I'm sorry, Emily. I've been away and just re-turned this morning."

"I had a notice put in the *Gazette*. Do you not read the papers when you're in London?"

"But I wasn't in London. Where I was, possession of an English newspaper might land you in gaol. You might even be executed."

Her eyes widened. "Are you saying you were in France?"

"What if I was?"

"Don't tease." She rose, started to pace. Impulse demanded that she should ask about her brothers, now. Brothers, who, according to Harold, had at one time been with Sir Lawrence's men. Who or what were Sir Lawrence's men, anyway? She should have asked Harold.

"Alex? Are you doing what your father was doing?"

"That depends on what you believe my father was doing."

"I don't know." She gave him an impatient look. "Nobody ever told me anything, and any interesting conversation the squire or the vicar had with Father always stopped the moment I was discovered.

"Poor Emily." Alex walked to the window, where the rain washed down the panes and obliterated any view of the drive and yard. He turned, leaning against the windowsill. "Cruel Emily. I am dead on my feet, yet I mustn't sit because the lady is bent on forging a path in my rug."

"It's not yet noon. How can you be tired?"

"Did I not say? I've just returned, and when you rang the bell, I was about to seek my bed."

She did see the shadows of fatigue beneath his eyes, but she also saw the glint of laughter accompanying the reference to his bed. Six years ago, she had been captivated by those laughing eyes, so in contrast with her father's stern gaze that always seemed to be tinged with disapproval. But, six years ago, Alex's ready laughter had not been inappropriate.

As if he'd read her mind, he said, "You used to like my teasing."

"Not when it is about your bed and my humiliation."

"Humiliation?" His mobile brows rose. "Whatever are you talking about?"

Striding past a credenza, she fought the urge to sweep every knickknack off the glossy mahogany top. "Dash it, Alex! I compromised myself, but I hoped you'd be a gentleman and not refer to my past foolishness.

"Be fair, Emily," he protested. "I said nothing about foolishness."

"It's not what you say, but *how* you say it. And I said *past* foolishness." She spun to face him and fiercely pronounced the baldest of lies. "And past it is, I promise you!"

"What a pity. I was very flattered that you had conceived such a passionate *tendre* for me."

"Indeed! If you were so flattered, why then did you send me packing?"

"Is that it?" He crossed to her in three long strides. "Darling misguided Emily! I may have many faults, but I do not seduce sixteen-year-old virgins."

"Don't patronize me or call me darling! And it was *I* who tried to seduce *you.*"

His mouth quirked. "I stand corrected. But if memory serves me right, did I not suggest that, once you'd gained a few years in age and experience, you might come back?" A careless finger caressed her cheek. "And here you are."

Breathless, she took a hasty step backward, out of his reach. As brief as his touch had been, her face felt aflame, and warmth was spreading throughout her body. But, no doubt, she assured herself, it was the effect of the brandy she'd quaffed.

"Alex, I came to see you for no other reason than to fulfill my father's wish."

He raised a brow. "Your father told you to visit me?"

"Did you know that I have brothers?" she countered.

Alex gave her a strange look.

"You do! You cannot deny it." She frowned. "But you make me feel positively doltish the way you look at me. As if I said something outlandish. Are you surprised that I was finally told about my brothers? Well, so was I."

"What precisely did your father tell you?"

"Personally, nothing. It was in his will. Father entrusted me with the search for my brothers, and he believed that the key to their whereabouts lies here, at Ravenhill."

"I see."

"Do you? That is more than I can say." She had the feeling of being led in a circle, and did not like it at all. "Alex, do you know where my brothers are, or do you not?"

"No, Emily. I don't know where your brothers are."

He sounded truthful. Sincere. And yet, there was something about his answer that bothered her. Or, perhaps, it was his expression. Guarded?

She took another step backward, brushed against a small round table. The chess table. She looked at the ivory and onyx pieces and wondered if they were still set out in the game disrupted by the dinner bell six years ago. Cousin Harold had come to fetch her and Alex because, Harold said, neither his mother nor Lady Raven would excuse them once more. Their absence at the luncheon table had been graciously overlooked, but not appearing to dinner would be considered beyond the pale.

She and Alex never finished that game. Instead, after dinner, Alex took her to the smugglers' cove. There was a full moon, and to Emily that walk with Alex seemed the most romantic and dashing thing to do. Of course Harold was supposed to have gone, too. But he stole away, preferring the mature charms of a serving wench in a Lydd tavern to the company of a gauche sixteen-year-old distant cousin.

Alex, though close to Harold's age, had treated Emily as a young lady. He made her feel grown-up. Beautiful. Worthy of attention. For two magical weeks. And she fell head over heels in love.

When they returned from the smugglers' cove that night, she thanked him, then, daringly, stood on tiptoe and kissed him on the cheek. His smile made her bones melt. He raised her hand to his lips, murmuring, "Darling little Emily. The pleasure was all mine."

And then he had kissed her.

"Emily!" Alex was waving another glass of brandy under her nose. "Dash it! That lightning strike must have rattled you more than I thought."

She hastily gathered her wayward thoughts. "I don't need more brandy. I am perfectly all right, thank you. And if you don't know anything about my brothers, then I shan't impose on you any longer. If you'll be kind enough to ring for Mary, I can be on my way. And you," she added brazenly, "may at long last seek your bed."

"You're too kind. But how far, darling Emily, do you think you'll get in this downpour?"

"Don't—" She broke off, the ever ready laughter in his eyes making her think twice about reprimanding him. If he wanted to call her darling Emily, he would, no matter what she said or how long she argued. Six years ago, she had delighted in their verbal sparring. And now—alas, she feared she would delight in it still. But she wasn't sixteen and innocent anymore.

She looked out the window, saw nothing but a thick, dark curtain of water, brightened every few seconds by flashes of lightning. She heard the thunder, all too close, and with stark misgivings resigned herself to her fate.

She unbuttoned her pelisse. Alex stepped forward to help her out of it, then dropped the garment carelessly on a sofa, where he had also set down the slim book with the tooled-leather cover and gold-lettered Latin inscription.

"Black becomes you, Emily. Most young ladies look colorless when they wear mourning. But with your dark hair and eyes, and with that golden-sand complexion I used to tease you about, you look—"

"Well?" she challenged when he fell silent. "How do I look?"

Something in his eyes changed as he looked her up and down. Gone was the laughter, replaced by a mixture of perplexity and awe. "You look exotic. An exotic beauty."

"Exotic!" she said, startled. "I never thought of the Marchmont coloring that way. But, I suppose, a Spanish ancestress who, in turn, had Moorish blood, could qualify me as exotic."

"No longer a young girl." He sounded as if he had made a great discovery. "You've grown up, Emily. You're a woman."

The warmth of his gaze was like a physical touch, gliding over her face, along her neck, the curve of her breasts, until her whole body was atingle.

Until she felt she'd do anything to be in his arms.

But she mustn't allow that sweet madness to cloud her reasoning again.

"Of course I'm a woman. What did you expect to happen in six years?"

"I don't know." He still sounded astonished and somewhat at a loss. "Perhaps I expected to see you again before now."

"Oh, you did, did you?" Irritation flared. "No doubt you came to Briar Cottage and were turned away? Or, perhaps, you wrote, but your letter went astray?"

He frowned, and she was once more aware of the signs of fatigue in his face, the shadows beneath his eyes, the lines etched sharply beside nose and mouth.

"Beg your pardon, Emily. I cannot seem to think straight. Need an hour, perhaps two, of sleep. Then I can once more converse intelligently."

"If I'm still here then." Gruffness concealed her feelings.

And what, precisely, were they, she wondered. But a moment ago, it was irritation; now, concern and a whole sleuth of other tender feelings she'd rather not explore. She was certain, though, that at sixteen she hadn't gone through such a seesaw of emotions.

But there was no doubt she'd still be here in two hours. Judging by the downpour, she might be marooned for the whole day—a thought that gave her a hollow feeling inside.

Abruptly, Emily turned away from Alex and started toward the door. "I had best check on Mary."

"I'll send for her."

"Quite unnecessary." She grasped the doorknob. "If you remember, I used to be a great favorite in the kitchens."

"Because you praised anything the cook offered, and because you could eat anytime."

"I could certainly eat something now," she said firmly. And it was comforting to know hunger could be blamed for the hollow feeling that would not abate.

"Emily?"

Opening the door, she turned to face him once more.

"Why did you come to see me?"

# THREE

"I told you. I came to inquire about my brothers."

"You could have written."

Emily frowned at Alex as he joined her at the door. "So I could have, I suppose. It never occurred to me."

"Did it not?" he asked softly.

"What do you mean? Oh—" Her face flamed. "You believe I came to see *you!* Dash it, Alex! I never realized how insufferably conceited you are."

"Yes, it is conceit, is it not? But I cannot deny that I did harbor such hopes—until I saw your indignation. I do beg your pardon, Emily, and freely admit that I'm a coxcomb."

She nodded in acknowledgment, but deep inside, she quaked. What was the truth? Why had it not occurred to her to write? She could not remember the precise wording of her father's will. Too much had been presented to her that day. Just yesterday. But, surely, she would never—on any pretext—have sought the opportunity to see Alex again, if such a meeting could have been avoided.

Or would she?

With all the dignity she could muster, she exited into the hall. "Go to bed, Alex. And rest assured that I have

come merely to honor my father's wish and to satisfy
my curiosity about my brothers and my mother."

"Your mother—now, there I can shed some light
immediately."

Emily spun. "Is she alive? Mr. Wordsworth did not
know."

"I'm sorry, Emily. Though she did not die twenty
years ago, as you were led to believe, she is dead now."

Strange, to feel a twinge of sadness, regret, when
she had lived with the certainty of her mother's death
for so long. "Did she die in—" Her throat was dry.
"In debtor's prison?"

Alex was about to reply when the sound of footsteps
made him look toward the rear of the hall. Two footmen approached. They stopped at some distance, the
younger staring at Emily with unabashed curiosity.
Catching her eye, he grinned, an impudence she recognized immediately. He was the same footman who
had sported a broken jaw and arm during her previous
visit. Even then, when he was quite obviously in discomfort, his grin and the irrepressible twinkle in his
dark eyes had made her want to smile back at him.
And she usually did, except when Cousin Harold or
his mother was nearby.

Alex gave the footmen a nod, then turned back to
Emily. "Your mother did not die in prison. Your father
had her released, and she died at Shoffield House in
Upper Grosvenor Street. Six years ago. Your father
was with her."

Startled, Emily said, "You must be mistaken. Father
stopped going to London when he could no longer
fit a boot on his gouty foot. And that was ten, eleven
years ago. I would remember—"

Her eyes widened. If her mother died six years ago . . .

"I was here, wasn't I?" she said. "It happened during my visit here at Ravenhill. I was astonished, but so proud and happy when the invitation from your parents arrived. My first visit anywhere." And the last. But that did not concern Alex.

She said, "It did not even bother me that I had to go with Cousin Harold and his mother. But it was a pretext, was it not? So I wouldn't know that Father was going up to London."

Alex's expression confirmed her suspicion. She took a few agitated steps, collected herself, and faced him with a semblance of calm.

"How *could* he, Alex? First, he led me to believe Mother died twenty years ago, then, so he won't have to tell me he's going to London to see her, he imposes on neighbors to invite me!"

"It was no imposition, Emily. Your father and my grandfather were as close as brothers. And my father used to be a frequent visitor at Shoffield Court."

"But not at Briar Cottage," she was quick to point out.

"No, not there. But don't you remember how much my mother enjoyed your visit? She was delighted with you."

Somehow, knowing that the invitation had been a pretext spoiled even the memory of Lady Raven's undeniable pleasure in the company of her young guest six years ago. "I know she missed your sister," Emily said quietly. "Canterbury may not be far, but it's not close enough for quick, impromptu visits."

Alex cupped her face in his palms, and she wanted

to capture his hands and keep them there, warm and firm against her skin. But he released her instantly.

He said, "I am sorry. You should have been told long ago. But your father would not; mine promised silence. Now that they're both dead, I feel no obligation to keep the truth from you, especially since already you seem to have heard some rumors about your mother."

"I'm glad you told me. At least I won't be tempted now to nourish false hopes." She met his gaze squarely and once again noted that something had changed in the way he looked at her. But she was not ready to examine what that change portended. "I only wish . . ."

"What, Emily? What do you wish?"

"That you could also give me the truth about my brothers."

He looked at her in silence. One of the footmen—Emily had quite forgotten about them—cleared his throat.

Alex said, "I don't know much about your brothers, Emily. But give me two hours' rest. Then we shall talk again."

Disappointment washed through her, but she did not let it show. She nodded, turned, started past the footmen toward the kitchen door at the back of the entrance hall, when suddenly she stopped and looked back. All three men were watching her.

"It's Frederick, isn't it?" she said to the younger footman. "How's your arm?"

His impudent grin was warm, familiar. "In fine trim, my lady. Need an arm to lean on or carry you, I'm your man."

"I thank you for the offer," she said gravely. "But I

hope I haven't reached the point of decrepitude in just six years."

With a smile and a wave, she continued on her way belowstairs, where Mary was undoubtedly enjoying a pot of tea and, perhaps, though it was a trifle early, one of the cook's delicious luncheons.

Alex watched until Emily had disappeared through the servants door, then closed his burning eyes and yawned hugely.

"One hour," he said to the footmen. "And bring food."

Without further ado, he bolted up the main stairway to seek the comfort and seclusion of his chambers. He did not ring for his man but tugged off his boots, loosened his cravat, and fell fully clothed onto the bed.

And then sleep deserted him.

Six years, since he last saw Emily. She had been a pretty child. Innocent and trusting. He'd known from the first day of her visit that she admired him. Admiration had quickly changed to infatuation. It was there, in her wide-eyed dark gaze, in her smile. He was three-and-twenty. Seven years her senior. But his mother made nothing of the girl's infatuation. Told him it was not at all surprising she should fancy herself in love. Not after having been sequestered with a misguided father, old enough to be her great-grandfather. Not when the only other young man she knew was Harold Marchmont.

His mother advised him to be kind to Emily, to treat her like a younger sister. That had been easy. His only sister—a termagant in his estimation—had recently married and left Ravenhill, and he was pleasantly surprised that, unlike Susan, Emily was always utterly delighted by any small attention he paid her.

He had not minded in the least devoting his time to her, especially since Harold went out of his way to display boredom in her company, and Mrs. Marchmont kept pinching at her about being too lively, too boisterous, too talkative, too everything. Besides, what else was he to do when his father had left him behind specifically to entertain the Lady Emily as a favor to Lord Shoffield.

Then came the night when he took Emily to the smugglers' cove. She had been in alt, thought it a splendid adventure. Since she hadn't the slightest notion of the Raven family's intimate knowledge of the "gentlemen" traders' dealings, she alternately quaked and thrilled at the possibility of encountering one of them. And when they were safely back home, she thanked him sincerely . . . then kissed him.

In truth, her part had been to touch her lips to his cheek in a chaste salute. Then *he* had done the kissing. And an unforgettable kiss it was. Her mouth was soft and warm and innocent. She wrapped her arms around his neck and kissed him back, totally trusting, totally giving.

It was her blatant inexperience that brought him to his senses. Feeling like a cad, he had gently set her free and belatedly resumed the role of older brother, telling her it was late, and she must be a good girl and run off to her bed.

Later, she had come to his bed.

Alex groaned. He never wanted to think of that encounter less than he did now. He was so tired, his eyes, his whole body, felt on fire.

Or, perhaps, it was memories that made him so dashed uncomfortable.

He rolled off the bed, stumbled to a chair, and fell into it. Why did she have to pick this, of all mornings, to seek him out? He had gone without sleep for three days and nights, had been shot at by the French and, almost home, by a patrol of revenue men. He needed to rest before conferring with the "Ravens," but rest was impossible in his bed—in this chamber of freshly wakened memories of a night six years ago . . .

He had been asleep and had not heard the door open, or heard her steps as she approached his bed. Neither had he felt her slipping beneath the covers. He was first aware of her as a pair of ice-cold feet against his leg, and when he turned, startled, he felt the softness of a female body.

"What the deuce!" He sat up, wide-awake and not a little astonished. He had never made advances to his mother's female staff, and he couldn't think of a single one bold enough to seek his bed uninvited. He clasped delicate, cotton-shrouded shoulders. "Who the devil are you?"

"Alex," she whispered. "It's me. Emily."

He let go of the shoulders as if they had turned into red-hot pieces of coal, leaped out of bed, and plunged into a pair of breeches.

"Emily, for goodness' sakes!" His hands shook as he fumbled with the tinder box, gave up, flung wide the drapes to let bright moonlight spill into the chamber. "What are you doing here?"

She sat up slowly, knelt in the middle of his bed, full-sleeved nightgown billowing around her, then settling against her body, hugging every delicate curve. Her dark hair tumbled down her back, almost to the waist. Wide-eyed, innocent, she gazed at him.

"Don't you want me here, Alex? I thought, when you kissed me . . . ? Would you kiss me again, please?"

He grew hot under that trusting, questioning look. "Emily, I shouldn't have kissed you. And you shouldn't be here. It puts us in a compromising position."

"I don't mind, Alex. If you don't? I only want to be with you."

A multitude of thoughts tumbled through his mind. Reason and emotions tangled in a knot. He paced. Raked his fingers through his hair. Nothing helped. Pacing didn't make order of the chaos in him.

"Alex?"

He faced her. "You're a child, Emily. You don't know what you're talking about."

She flinched, as if he'd struck her a physical blow. And he hurt for her.

"I'm sorry." He stepped to the bed. "I'm bungling this quite thoroughly. What I meant is that you're too young to think of love."

She gave him a long look, then, with touching dignity, climbed off his bed.

Desire to take her in his arms, to hold her, washed over him so strongly it scared him to the depth of his soul. Tarnation! He was three-and-twenty. A man of the world. A "Raven" not only in name, but in deed. He ought to be able to deal with this. To say just the right words to make her feel better.

He forced a grin, flicked her chin with a careless finger. "You shouldn't be in such a hurry, you know. Before long, a platoon of men will be fighting over you. That's when you must take your pick. Not when your choice is between your cousin and me."

"Good night, Alex. I am sorry I disturbed you." With a slight inclination of her head, she moved toward the door.

Something in him knotted painfully. He caught up to her, caressed that long, dark, silky hair. Just once.

"Darling Emily. You don't know what a treasure you are."

She stood quite still, face averted. In a voice so low, he could scarcely hear it, she said, "Thank you, Alex."

Her quietness, so unlike her lively self, was unnerving.

"Emily, if I hurt you . . . I swear it wasn't my intent."

She looked at him then, and her smile was as bright as any smile she had ever given him. "Don't worry about me, Alex. As you say, I'll have dozens of suitors when I'm a little more grown-up."

"That's the ticket!" He grinned back, almost light-headed with relief to see her cheerful again. And what, for an instant, he believed to be tears, could only be a reflection of the moonlight in her dark eyes. "Who knows, Emily? When you're a little more experienced in the ways of the world, you may even want to come back to Ravenhill and show me what a fool I was."

"Yes. I suppose I might do that. Good night, Alex."

She opened the door—and walked straight into the arms of Lydia and Harold Marchmont . . .

When someone rapped sharply on his bedroom door, Alex stirred, realized he was slumped in a chair, and had scarcely straightened his aching back before

the door swung open. Frederick, no longer in footman's livery but sporting leather breeches and a riding coat, entered with a laden tray.

"Rise and shine, Raven." Frederick set the tray
down and poured coffee. "Here's some Turkish brew
to help you rouse your brains. And you'll need all of
them. The Lady Emily has had time to reflect and is
chomping at the bit to ask you more questions."

Alex accepted the cup. He frowned at Frederick's
attire. "Change in plans? Where are you off to?"

"No change. I'm only fetching Rose and the little
ones before they're marooned."

"Still bad out?" Alex craned his stiff neck to catch
a glimpse out the window. He heard no more thunder,
but the rain was a veritable waterfall. "Which means,
we'll all be marooned *here.* Including Emily. There's
no way I can send her back across the marsh."

"The hand of fate, you might say."

"Aye," said Alex, thinking of Emily as she had been
led away by Lydia Marchmont six years ago, while
Harold confronted him and suggested a speedy marriage. Although the notion held appeal—in fact, more
appeal than he cared to admit—he had just as coldly
informed Harold Marchmont that nothing had happened. That, assuredly, he would not take advantage
of the situation by marrying a trusting, inexperienced
child simply because her cousin's mind was as filthy
as the taverns he frequented.

"So, my lord Shoffield is dead, is he?" said Frederick
with an impudent grin. They had known each other
since adolescence, and Frederick, a few years the senior, had led Alex into many an innocent and not so
innocent scrape. "And the Lady Emily is looking for
her brothers."

"Will you tell her?" asked Alex.

"Hardly my place, is it?" Frederick sauntered to the door. "I'll be off, then. Good luck with the Lady Emily."

# FOUR

Good luck?

Alex stopped halfway down the stairs. Just what the deuce had Frederick meant by it?

He had no time for reflection. Emily appeared at the foot of the stairs. Arms akimbo, she looked up at him.

"You said two hours, Alex! It's been close on three. What have you been doing all this time?"

"Eating. Bathing. Shaving. Dressing. Let me see, what have I forgotten?"

"Oversleeping!"

"No, not that. In truth, I hardly slept at all." He descended slowly, his eyes never leaving her face. "Memories, darling Emily. They kept me awake."

She said nothing.

"Six years ago, I considered myself a man of the world who handled a delicate situation with great aplomb. I realize now that I was a graceless clod and a fool. Did I hurt you very much, Emily?"

They faced each other at the foot of the stairs. Emily had turned a little pale, but her gaze did not falter.

"Yes, I was hurt," she said quietly. "At the time, I believed it was you who hurt me. But as I grew older and wiser, I began to understand that I had caused the pain myself by going to your chamber.

"No. The fault was mine. You were too young . . . grew up without a mother to advise you."

"I had a governess. A very good one." Her smile was rueful. "That year following my visit here, I almost wished I wasn't growing wiser. Your rejection hurt, but it seemed mild compared to the agony of humiliation I suffered when I realized what an utter fool I'd been."

"No! Listen to me, Emily." He clasped her hands, held them against his chest. "*I* was the fool."

Emily scarcely heard him. She felt the rise and fall of his chest, the warmth of his hands around hers, and felt all the wisdom gained in six years slipping rapidly away. His head was bent close to hers, the hair still slightly damp and slicked down, and she wanted to run her fingers through it and restore the unruly, wayward look it had when dry.

She drew away sharply. "No more talk about the past, Alex. It's over and done with."

"Is it? Don't misunderstand, I want your hurt to be a thing of the past. But I very much wish—" It was Alex, who raked his fingers through his hair. "Dash it, Emily! I wish I had done the right thing six years ago. Actually, two things. And the first, I can rectify immediately."

With that, he swept her into his arms. His mouth claimed hers in a kiss that robbed her of breath and reason. She had no will, except to respond to the demands of that mouth, alternately ruthless and fiery, tender and coaxing. It was the kiss of her most secret dreams, a need at last fulfilled, and she could no more deny her own passion than she could deny her delight in his.

When, at last, he set her free to draw a ragged breath, she still clutched his coat sleeves in a grip so hard she could feel her nails digging through the fabric into her palms.

"Emily." He kissed her nose. "Darling Emily. I—"

"No!" She pushed him away. "Don't say anything. I don't know what I would want to hear. All I know is that I could not leave at present, even if I wished it. Therefore, I should very much like to pretend that nothing happened just now."

He gave her a long, searching look. At last he nodded, saying amiably, "Of course, Emily. If that is what you wish."

"I do!" Her voice was firm, her resolution strong. Alas, she knew quite well that it would be impossible, at least for her, to forget what happened.

Alex said, "It's dashed uncomfortable standing about in the hall, don't you think? A fire should be laid in the front room by now."

"Begging your pardon, Sir Alex. Lady Emily." One of three footmen stepping out from nowhere, or so it seemed, and lugging huge baskets of wood, grinned at Emily in a manner reminiscent of the footman Frederick. "We're running a bit behind, it appears. But we'll have a fire going in no time at all."

The three bowed to Emily, who found herself torn between relief and displeasure at the interruption. The men carried their loads to the ten-foot fireplace in the hall.

"I say, Martin!" Alex followed them. "We don't want a fire here. Lay it in the front room."

"Chimney's blocked in the front room.

An almost imperceptible frown, gone as soon as it appeared, flitted across Alex's face. "It is? Since when?"

"Quite recently," said Martin, once more displaying his cocky grin.

"Well, then. It can't be helped, can it?" Alex sounded unaccountably cheered. He joined Emily. "We don't use this fireplace much. It's mainly for the yule log. But—" A careless shrug. "If the one in the front room smokes . . ."

"The front room is not the only sitting room you have." Emily watched him through narrowed eyes. "What's going on, Alex?"

The old, familiar laughter glinted in his eyes, though his face remained quite straight. "The smoking chimney? Dashed if I know what's amiss. Mother orders the chimneys swept quite frequently."

"Fiddlesticks! I'm not speaking of chimneys." She pointed an accusing finger. "You looked like that when you told Cousin Harold your mother's maids all had some strange disease, when it was obvious they weren't ill at all, and you said it only to keep Harold from sneaking after them!"

This shook him, but only momentarily. "I hope it was shamefaced I looked, if I fibbed so blatantly."

"You did not look the least bit shamefaced. And *now,* you're grinning. As are your footmen!"

He raised a quizzical brow. "Are we too friendly and casual at Ravenhill, Lady Emily?"

She frowned at the three men, who had lit the fire and, at her look, busied themselves stacking the remaining logs in a huge iron wood-cradle.

"You were casual six years ago." All of a sudden, she found herself wondering what the second thing was that he wished he had done right, six years ago.

Lud! She was staring at him like a moonling. Briskly, she said, "Your free and easy ways did not bother me then. They would not now. Except—you see, it's the number of footmen that's been nagging at me. Three here. Then there was Frederick and the other one."

"That was George. Frederick and George. These fine, strapping men are Martin—" Alex motioned with his hand. "Christopher, and Hugh."

"Six years ago, you had only Frederick. And Martin, why, he has the same impudent grin as Frederick. They *all* look a bit like Frederick."

"They're brothers."

Her breath caught. "Alex?"

"Yes, Emily?"

In the face of his blandness, the raised brow, she could not ask. Could not voice the sudden stab of suspicion. Surely, she was quite wrong.

Footmen?

Once more, she looked at them. The man named Martin seemed about Frederick's age, somewhere between thirty and five-and-thirty. Christopher and Hugh were somewhat older.

They picked up the empty baskets, bowed, and marched off.

"What are you thinking, Emily?"

She gave Alex a pensive look. "Once, I would have told you instantly."

"But now, you don't trust me."

"You'll laugh."

"Are you afraid of a little laughter, Emily? You did not use to be that timid."

"You're laughing at me altogether too much."

"Not *at* you, Emily." Clasping her shoulders, he looked at her with such sincerity that she could not doubt him. "It's this dashed situation in which I find myself. I cannot explain. Not just now. But we used to think so much alike, to feel alike. Could you not trust me once more, and believe that my laughter is not directed *at* you?"

She stepped back, when she wanted to do just the opposite, wanted to be in his arms and forget about her pesky brothers, her father's will. She wanted to ask Alex about himself, why he wasn't married—

"I know you well enough to see that you're trying to pull the wool over my eyes . . . and I'm convinced it is to do with my brothers. Harold said they joined your father's men. He said they were—" Emily swallowed. "Guillotined in Paris. But Father believed the report was false."

"Something is certainly false. None of my father's men were ever guillotined."

She looked at him, waited for more. When the silence stretched, she tapped an impatient foot.

"Dash it, Alex! I don't know why I ever took such delight in conversing with you. Trying to get information from you is like trying to milk a dry cow."

He burst out laughing. "And do you speak from experience, Emily?"

"It's what our housekeeper says, and she comes from a family of dairy farmers. But what does it matter? Alex, you're as slippery as an eel—and, yes, I do speak from personal experience! Why are you so reluctant to talk about my brothers? If they were with Sir Lawrence's men—whatever or whoever those men were—"

"Smugglers."

"I beg your pardon?"

"Smugglers," he repeated obligingly. "Sir Lawrence's men—actually, Sir Alexander's men, now. My men. The 'Ravens.' They are smugglers."

"Then it's true. I caught a whisper once, but I thought I must have misheard."

"You did not."

Her mind whirled with the implications. Then, irrelevantly, she remembered something else. Something that had her flush with indignation. "When you took me to the smugglers' cove, you knew all along there wasn't any danger of encountering the freetraders, didn't you? But you let me run on and on about what we should do if they suddenly showed up."

"Unfair, Emily. You did not believe me when I said the full moon would keep us safe."

"Because it has been known to happen. That they show up at full moon! It has, you know."

"Indeed, it has," he agreed solemnly.

"And, no doubt, you enjoyed every time I jumped at a slight noise!"

"Only because I believed *you* enjoyed it."

She drew breath for an indignant reply, then shook her head and smiled. "It was, indeed, splendid fun. Dash it, Alex! I was such a goose back then."

"A delightful goose, darling Emily."

Her smile faded. She started to pace, her panacea for every uncomfortable emotion from irritation to restlessness, impatience, embarrassment, agitation, and a great many others.

She looked at Alex from a distance. "And Harold was correct? My brothers worked with your father? And now, Alex? Do they work with you?"

He hesitated.

"Alex?"

"Yes, Lord Shoffield's sons are working with me."

"Where are they?"

"Around. Emily—"

The door to the front sitting room opened and a gentleman strolled into the hall. His dark blue coat was damp around the collar and the sleeves, his boots and buckskins were spattered with mud. In his hand he carried a slim book that looked very much like the volume Alex had held when he opened the front door for Emily.

Her breath caught as she took in the gentleman's dark hair, liberally streaked with silver, the dark eyes, aquiline nose, the firm set of mouth and chin, so like—

"I must beg pardon, my dear," he said, bowing to her. "But I've been eavesdropping quite shamelessly and realize I must rescue Alex from a dilemma."

"About time!" said Alex, joining them. "I was beginning to fear I'd have to force your hand."

The other man paid him no heed but kept his eyes on Emily. "My name is Edward Marchmont."

"I knew it." She felt strangely numb and breathless, and terribly excited. "You look just like Father in his prime . . . the way he looked in the portrait that shows him with his hunter."

"So I've been told." Edward gave a slight smile. "You, I'm glad to see, have escaped the Marchmont nose."

"Lud!" She drew a shaky breath. "How strange this is! I finally meet my brother—one of them—and I don't know what to say!"

"My dear, you are mistaken. I'm not your brother. I am your father."

# FIVE

Emily did not consider herself the swooning type of female, but she was perilously close to fainting now. At least, if Alex had not caught her around the waist, she would have sat down flat on the cold marble floor. But with his arm supporting her, she made it safely to a bench facing the fireplace, though her head kept spinning.

"Yes," she heard Alex say, and for some reason, his arm was still around her waist, and he was seated beside her. "That's just what she needs. Hand it over, Hugh."

Alex held a glass to her lips, but she pushed it away. She did not, however, push Alex away. She needed him, his solid strength. In a moment, she'd get up and walk off the strange flutter of nerves. But right at present, she did not feel up to taking a single step.

She looked about her, saw not only Edward Marchmont, but also four footmen gazing at her. Footmen at Ravenhill always seemed to be readily at hand. All were solemn, except Martin, who winked at her.

She met Edward Marchmont's kind and slightly troubled eyes. "If you're my father, then . . . ?" She looked at the footmen.

"They're your uncles," said Edward. "Two of us are not present. Frederick, who is the youngest. And

John, the third eldest. Between John and me is George, here."

One of the men, a little portly, rather grave—she had seen him with Frederick earlier—stepped forward and bowed over her hand.

"Then we have Hugh," said Edward.

"It's a pleasure, niece." Hugh's smile was marred slightly by a thin scar running from the corner of his mouth to the jawbone.

"Christopher and Martin."

A friendly grin, and an impudent one. Two firm handshakes.

Questions whirled through her mind. She could not focus on a single one.

Edward said, "You probably wonder . . . suspect . . . but be assured, your mother and I knew each other *before* she married Father. We intended to wed. Margret was—" He paused, ran a finger inside his collar as if it was too tight. "She was already with child, you see. But when I introduced her to Father, she decided to marry him instead."

Even seated, Emily was once more glad of Alex's supporting arm. Not that she was scandalized to hear Margret and Edward had been lovers; though, perhaps, she should be. But she understood all too well, and it was the thought of her own narrow escape six years ago that made her feel weak. She did not understand, however, why Margret would have jilted Edward.

"It makes no sense. Why did she want to marry my fath—*your* father instead of you?"

Hands behind his back, Edward started to pace—as Emily did so often. She waited, certain that, in a moment, when he had gathered his thoughts, he would continue the tale.

He was an imposing figure, elegant despite the mud on his boots. Indeed, he was the image of her father—heavens, nay! Of her *grandfather* in his prime.

Alex spoke softly into her ear. "Shall I ring for tea? Sherry? Emily, you're so still, it worries me."

"I am very well, thank you." She gave in to a craving to nestle deeper into the warmth of his wide shoulder. "Besides, you don't need to ring. You have a bevy of footmen standing by."

"Baggage," he whispered.

She heard the smile in his voice but made no reply. Edward Marchmont had stopped pacing.

George gave him a friendly clap on the back, then retreated to prop a shoulder against the mantelpiece. Hugh, Christopher, and Martin joined him there, as if to show Edward that, although he was on his own in this first encounter with his daughter, he was not alone. He had his brothers at his back.

Edward said, "This is not a pretty tale, Emily."

"I do not expect it. Only the truth."

"After meeting Father, Margret told me she had no desire to wait a decade or two to become a countess. Neither did she wish to live on the paltry income to which the viscountcy entitled me. She said Father knew she was *enceinte* and would acknowledge the child as his." Again, Edward tugged at his collar. "But she had not told him. He did not learn the truth until you were two years old."

"Did you tell him, then?"

Edward was silent for so long that Emily was about to repeat her question, when Martin said, " 'Twas Margret herself, who told Father. She was in one of her peevish moods, and—"

"Hush, Martin!" Edward cast him a look that put Emily in mind of the stern, unbending man she had believed to be her father all these years. "This is not your tale to tell."

"Oh, isn't it?" Impudent grin replaced by a scowl, Martin strode forward. "And why not, pray tell? Margret's poisonous tongue had Father believe that any and all of us could be the child's father. Even me, who was but fifteen at the time Margret conceived! The deuce! I'm surprised she did not name Frederick. He was a ripe old twelve and at Eton when she first cast out her lures to you."

Stunned, Emily sat on the bench. She ought to slap Martin as she had slapped Cousin Harold when he disparaged her mother. But something stopped her, and it wasn't Alex's arm tightening around her. Rather, it was the direction of Edward Marchmont's anger as he strictured his brother—not for slandering Margret but for distressing Emily with the harsh truth.

Edward turned back to her. "I beg your pardon. As I said, not a pretty tale, but there is no need to overwhelm you, for I doubt you've heard anything at all about the affair from Father. I saw your notice in the Gazette, and let me add right now that I feel it would be wise if he remained your father. He acknowledged you, and you grew up as his child. If we change that now, it'll be you who suffers."

"Very sensible," said Hugh. "I doubt Eliza would be pleased if the scandal broth thickened too much around our name. It'll cause enough of a stir to have all of us reappear, but Gussy will need to come out next year."

"Who," Emily said faintly, "are Eliza and Gussy?"

Hugh stepped closer. "My wife and daughter. I also have two sons, ten and thirteen years old. They are in Lydd."

"Gracious." Aware of the inadequacy of her reply, Emily asked, "Are you the only one who's married?"

Another of her uncles—Christopher—chuckled. "Staggered, are you, niece? But there's Frederick, who's gone to fetch his wife and two strapping lads of two and four. I have a wife and son in Rye. The only ones who never married are Martin and John."

"There's hope for me yet," Martin said cheerfully. "I'm only five-and-thirty, and none of you were inclined to marry young."

"Aye. But John—" Christopher shook his head. "He's going on fifty, and the only woman he's ever loved was Josephine Bonaparte. Now he's buried his heart in books. He's the Archbishop of Canterbury's bibliothecary."

George said gravely, "I lost my family in France."

"I am sorry." Emily would have liked to learn more about John and Josephine or ask what happened to George's family, but George, apparently, had said all he would say at present, for he stooped and busied himself replenishing the wood in the grate.

She was beginning to feel more like her old self, no longer faint or overwhelmed. And that, she reluctantly acknowledged, meant she must no longer indulge in the comfort of Alex's arm encircling her waist.

Alex, who, like the Marchmont men, had made no move to marry young.

Abruptly, she rose. "Father had a report that all of you died in France. Why did you never set him straight? Why did you break off all contact with him?"

Edward pocketed the book he carried, then took her hand, holding it in both of his. "My dear, there'll be time enough to explain everything. Suffice it to say—for now, at least—that extremely harsh words were exchanged because our father believed . . ."

When Edward faltered, Emily said, "Don't spare my feelings, I beg you. I suspect he accused you of dallying with Mother even after she'd married him? He often perceived a slight or wrong when none was offered."

"If it had been only me he accused! And nothing we said could convince him otherwise!" Edward's mouth tightened. Then he smiled at her. "But enough of that. We left Shoffield Court. That must have satisfied him."

"Did you come straight here, to Ravenhill?"

"We did. Sir Lawrence was a close friend. He was also a government man, and we joined him."

*A government man! A spy.* Emily glanced quickly at Alex, who had gone to speak with Martin and George. Alex did not catch her look, but Edward noticed.

He said, "Yes, Alex works for the War Office. He took over when Sir Lawrence died. That's why he's gone so much. The first few years, he and Frederick were too young, of course, and stayed behind with Lady Raven and her daughter. Father must have suspected what we did. When he moved with you to Briar Cottage, he came to Ravenhill asking about us. But we had a pact with Lawrence and his wife: not a word about us to Father."

Emily was thinking about Margret, Countess of Shoffield—her mother—and the rumor that she'd run off with one of her husband's sons. "Did Mother leave Shoffield Court with you?"

"No."

"But she did leave. Do you know why?"

"No."

"Emily has the right to know, old boy." Hugh gave his brother a severe look, then turned to Emily. "You'd better have it from us than from some old gossip when you're in London."

"I've heard rumors already, but I'd rather have the truth."

Edward said, "We know nothing about it. Only what Father told Lady Raven after Margret's death, and what Sir Lawrence heard in London."

"That will suffice," Emily said quietly.

Edward released her hands, paced. "It appears that Margret had fallen in love with a scarlet coat. Some stripling officer, home on sick leave. When he returned to his regiment, she went with him. Followed the drum."

Hugh muttered, "Changed protectors as a man may change his shirt."

Feeling herself go cold with dread, Emily looked from one man to the other. Her mother . . . a fallen woman.

Hugh mumbled an apology, turned away.

Edward faced her. "Your mother wasn't a bad woman. But very restless. Unhappy, I think. She lived in Paris during the Peace of Amiens. I saw her once, though she did not see me. Some day I will tell you all I know. But I must hurry off. I have news to take to London." He patted his coat pocket. "And I must stop with John for a translation."

"I tried my hand at it," said Alex, strolling up to them. "But Latin was never my strong suit. Besides, I was too dashed tired."

Emily tore her mind from the chilling tale of her

mother's life and looked at Alex in sudden understanding. "The book with the Latin inscription you
carried when you opened the door for me! You
brought it from France."

"Smuggled goods. From a priest, no less. Told you
the 'Ravens' are smugglers, didn't I?"

The laughter in Alex's eyes warmed Emily's heart.
But she must not pay attention to her heart. It could
only lead her astray.

Edward said, "For the past three years, I've worked
out of London. The War Office. I traveled down with
my wife and daughters, but when the storm broke, I
left them in Lydd with Hugh's family. They'll be here
presently—"

"Or not," cut in Alex when thunder could once
more be heard.

"I have sisters?" Wide-eyed, Emily confronted Edward. "Why did you not tell me immediately? How old
are they? What are their names?"

"Dominique and Gabrielle are seventeen. They're
twins." Edward once more possessed himself of her
hand. "Antoinette, my wife, knows the truth. My
daughters, however, will look upon you as their aunt.
I beg you—"

"Yes, of course . . . brother. I wish you God speed,
Edward. And do not worry. I shall love my nieces and
their mother. *All* my new relations!"

He nodded, but still held her hand. "Just once, if
you permit, I will call you daughter and clasp you to
my heart."

Blinking away a sudden rush of tears, Emily smiled
and found herself caught to her father's breast. He
held her for a long moment, then kissed her forehead.

"I shall see you again soon, Emily." Without a back-

ward look, he strode off, calling to his brothers to provide him with oilskins and a dry pair of boots. The
four obligingly followed him to the back of the hall.

Emily looked at Alex. "I'd hoped at least one of
them would stay and talk to me."

"There will be ample time later on." Alex seemed
distracted, his brow creased in thought, his gaze directed at the men disappearing through the servants
door. "Judging by the sound of the storm, you won't
be leaving any time soon."

"Alex—"

"Emily, will you excuse me?" He looked to be in a
great rush all of a sudden, already turning and starting
to move away. "There's something I should tell Edward."

"Why, of course, sir," she said to his back and trying
to quash the feeling of being deserted. "I wouldn't
dream of detaining you."

And then she sat down on the bench in front of the
vast fireplace to contemplate the merrily dancing
flames in lonely splendor.

She had found the men she came to seek. Her
brothers, who turned out to be her father and her
uncles and yet, in the eyes of the world, would remain
her brothers forevermore.

Well, that did not matter. Father, brothers, or uncles, they were all close kin. She would get to know
them and their families, and love them. And, she
hoped, would be loved in return.

Heady news for one who had believed herself alone,
except for a disagreeable distant cousin—who must
now forget about succeeding to the title. It was Edward
who was the new Earl of Shoffield. For a long moment,
Emily basked in happy thoughts about this vast family

she had acquired. Family to visit, to share laughter and tears.

Tears . . . they did come. All too soon. But no one with whom to share.

Tears for her mother.

She'd never know what had driven Margret to first cast off the father of her child, then to desert husband and daughter.

Or why she had chosen the life of a courtesan above that of a wife and mother. And six years ago . . . Alex had not denied that Margret was in debtor's prison until her husband had her released, so that she might die at Shoffield House. Surely Margret could have turned to her husband before she ended up in such dire straits.

Unless she considered herself beyond redemption? A fallen woman.

And Emily was her mother's daughter.

"Emily?"

She rose from the bench, looked at Alex, and started to pace. She had no notion of passage of time. He might have been gone a few minutes or several hours.

"Will you lend me a mount, Alex?"

His expression, quite set and purposeful when he first addressed her, changed to comic dismay. "I know our hall is as vast as the arena at Astley's. But, Emily! Think of the marble!"

She scowled at him. "Very funny."

He watched her pace. Serious, now, he said, "Even on horseback you'd find it nigh impossible to get home."

"Edward is riding!"

"He does not need to cross the marsh. He's going to Canterbury. What's the hurry, Emily? But a few moments ago, you could not wait to have more speech with your . . . brothers."

"Indeed, my brothers." She stopped, faced him. "And you certainly did your best to pull the wool over my eyes. I should be cross with you, Alex!"

"But you're not. You understand that I found myself in a deucedly ticklish situation. I knew the truth, but it wasn't my place to tell you."

"And Frederick! To think that I met him six years ago, and he never said a word. But he knew. No wonder he was forever grinning at me. I shall have to comb his hair with a joint-stool!"

Alex merely smiled, and it was as if the years slipped back and she was sixteen once more and experienced the impact of that bone-melting smile for the first time. She took a hasty step backward, stumbling a little and clutching at the bench for support.

"Emily—" His eyes caressed her. "Aren't you at all curious what I had to say to Edward?"

But she had only one thought. "I must get back to Briar Cottage!"

"Why?"

"If I don't leave now, I may be stranded for the night. Then, what would I do?"

"Stay here, of course."

"No, Alex! It wouldn't do at all." Not as long as she felt about him exactly as she did six years ago.

"Darling Emily, why do you look so panic-stricken? You have your maid. You have uncl—brothers. Frederick's wife will be here momentarily. Surely that is sufficient chaperonage?"

She retreated another step, folded her arms across her middle to hide her shaking hands. "I must leave."

"You cannot. Emily, hear me out, please." He advanced. "I mean to do this properly. Give me your hand."

"My hand?" Instinctively, she clutched her arms tighter.

"I shall need it, if I am to make you an offer in style."

Her breath caught. "An offer . . . of *marriage*?"

"What else?" The laughter was back in his eyes. "You don't think I'd approach Edward if I had something less in mind?"

"Alex, this is not a good time to be roasting me!"

"Roasting you! Nothing is further from my mind. Emily, you cannot be surprised. When I kissed you, surely you understood I'd be asking you. And your response—dash it! You wouldn't convince me you were shamming it if you swore on your mother's soul."

Her mouth was dry, and she was cold from the inside out. Her mother's soul . . . how ironic.

"Alex, you kissed me six years ago. Naively, I dreamed of marriage then. Even when Lydia and Harold whisked me away the next morning on some pretext that Father sent for me—"

"No pretext. Your father did send a note signaling he had returned from London."

She brushed the interjection aside. "Even after we left, I still dreamed you'd follow me and declare yourself. Harold very soon put an end to that foolish notion. He told me he demanded marriage and you bluntly refused."

"I refused because I would have been taking advantage of you." Alex raked his fingers through his hair.

"You were too young. Your father had kept you in virtual seclusion. You knew no other young men."

"I still don't. And if you're trying to tell me those selfless, noble reasons were the only ones that kept you from making an offer, then pray explain why you did not once call on me." She raised a challenging brow. "Or write."

"I was in France, Emily. Frederick and I followed the rest of the 'Ravens' just as soon as your carriage was out the gates. I ended up staying in France. Four and a half years. You must have noted that I was absent from my father's funeral?"

Her heart was pounding. "How could I have known? Father did not attend the funeral because of his gout. And he did not consider it seemly for me to go. But never mind that. The past is irrelevant."

"Aye," he agreed warmly. "I was surprised to hear you bring it up. And if you'll give me your hand now, I'll kiss it, and drop to my knees and propose in style."

"Don't!" She turned away. "I could not accept your offer. Alex, do but consider!"

In the sudden silence, the crackle and hiss of the fire sounded loud, intrusive.

Then Alex stood before her. "Darling Emily, I know you've had a harrowing day, and—"

"Not at all! It is a splendid day. A fairy-tale day. Where else but in a fairy tale does a girl set out to seek her brothers, and finds a father and uncles instead?"

"I agree." His voice caressed. "But a true fairy tale must also have a couple that will live happily ever after."

"It cannot be us. Don't you see?" Once more, she turned her back on him. It was so very difficult to speak when every word she uttered was contrary to what she wanted to say. "When I visited your room—"

"Don't!" he cut in. He clasped her shoulders from behind. "Don't think it started you on the path your mother chose!"

"I do not. Though it was most improper of me. Scandalous, in fact. But I don't see myself seeking . . . protectors, as Mother apparently did. Rather, I fear it is the reason you want to propose. You said earlier that you wished you had done the right thing six years ago."

Alex wrapped his arms around her. When he spoke, his mouth was close to her ear. "No, indeed," he said softly. "There'll be no protectors for you, darling Emily. But as for the reason I want to marry you—" His arms tightened around her. "You're way off the mark if you think it's some belated sense of duty."

Once more, there was a silence that magnified every small sound in the vast hall, including, Emily feared, the wild hammering of her pulse.

Slowly, she turned in his arms. A quick look confirmed that he was quite serious. She liked it better when he laughed at her; it made it easier to use a rallying tone.

Placing her hands against his chest, she pushed away a little. Gaze fixed firmly on the sapphire pin nestled in the folds of his cravat, she inquired a trifle breathlessly, "What other reason could you possibly have?"

"Love?" he offered.

Her eyes flew to his face. "Alex, if you're saying you fell in love with me today, I shan't believe you!"

"No, darling Emily. Today, I finally *recognized* that I love you."

While she still searched his face with painful intensity, he drew her close—and her world was put to rights. He was warmth and strength and solidity. He was the dream she had dreamed for six long years, and before she could utter a word, his mouth claimed hers in a kiss that answered all her unspoken questions and laid to rest any lingering doubts.

At last, he held her at arm's length. "There," he said a little unsteadily. "Was that reason enough for me to propose?"

"Yes." Her voice was as shaky as his. "I daresay it was."

"And reason enough for you to accept?"

"Yes. Oh, yes!"

"Then let us get married as soon as we can. Emily, you won't insist on waiting out the mourning period, will you?"

"No. But, Alex—"

"Good." He kissed the corners of her mouth, her eyes. "If I haven't told you yet, I love you, darling Emily. And I asked Edward to send down John with a special license from the archbishop. Now, was there something you wished to say?"

"I love you, Alex."

And what did it matter that he had not actually made a formal offer when, instead, he kissed her once again and gave her a small but very delicious sampling of Happily Ever After.

# THE EMPEROR'S NIGHTINGALE

by
**Judith A. Lansdowne**

# ONE

Once upon a time in a rather small portion of England bounded on the south by the English Channel and on the north by Weaver's Meadows, snuggled beneath a hill from which—if one had the time and patience to climb it—one might gaze upon Cornwall and glittering far off in the distance, the Atlantic Ocean—a tiny Empire thrived. It was not truly an Empire, but everyone who knew of it called it such because the gentleman whose word was law there, the Duke of Amber, had had the great misfortune to be named by his mama—his papa having died before his birth and thus being unable to protest—Julius Caesar Crofton. Well, not even his nurse could resist that, and so he was dubbed The Emperor right from the first—though no one ever addressed him as such or made the least reference to it when his mama was present. Necessarily then, his ducal seat, the lands running with it, and the village to its east, grew to be called in certain circles The Empire of Amber.

The Emperor grew to be a slender, broad-shouldered gentleman with eyes of soft and misty violet and hair the color of rich molasses. And though he often developed the most exceptional desires and grew quite accustomed to having every whim fulfilled, he nonetheless was generally regarded as a most unassuming and thoughtful person and was held in fond admiration by his servants, his relatives and his friends.

Almost more than anything—riding or dancing or simply fiddling about town—The Emperor liked to read. And what he liked to read the most were books and stories and poems about his ducal seat, which had always been a most extraordinary place and had been visited and remarked upon by dignitaries and scholars and wealthy and important people from all over the world. An architectural anomaly born whole from the imagination of the very first Duke of Amber, the Emperor's great-great-great-great (oh, any number of greats) grandfather, the house itself was called Bright—not Bright Hall or Bright Court or Bright Grange or Bright Castle—just Bright, and that was all.

Erected with bricks that had once been mere sand-colored clay, but had become mixed in the kiln and fired with gold and silver, quartz and iron, manganese and cobalt and any number of gemstones, the outer walls of Bright glistened and glowed and sparked like fireworks in the sunlight. Glittering first red then gold then blue then green then crystal, depending upon the angle from which one approached and the fickleness of the sun, the first sight of that splendid house could not but stop every visitor in his tracks and steal his breath completely away.

All around Bright the sweetest and finest and rarest and most beautiful flowers grew. Cobbled paths had been laid down among them and stone benches set, so that one might sit and watch the flowers grow if that was what one desired. And to each of the flowers in Bright's gardens, as soon as it had grown tall enough, the gardener tied a tiny silver bell, so that whenever the wind blew through the Empire of Amber, the bells would chime and charm every heart that heard them. Beyond the flower gardens, which stretched so far in all directions that The Emperor himself had never strolled through all of them, lay a meadow through which a stream meandered, and beyond the meadow, a wood, and in that wood dwelt the most extraordinary nightingale.

This nightingale sang so sweetly that even the woodcutter in the midst of his chopping could not help but stop and listen to her. He would lean his axe against the trunk of a tree and doff his cap and swipe with his sleeve at the sweat upon his brow. Then he would sink down onto the ground and close his eyes and listen to the sweetness of her song. And when she had finished, he would look up to find her sitting upon a branch above him and ask her, "Will ye not sing ta me agin, sweet bird?" And the nightingale would nod and sing to him once more, and then the woodcutter would be easy in his mind and return to his work with a deal more energy and a lighter heart. Truly, there was no sound so fine in all the world as the sound of that nightingale perched among the branches singing of love and of life, of joy and of sorrow—singing all of the songs of all of the hearts of all of the people in all of the Empire of Amber.

Every year since The Emperor had reached his majority, a veritable army of visitors could be counted upon to appear at Bright beginning in June and ebbing and flowing through the house like a tide, until winter's frost discouraged the most of them. Invited by the dowager duchess, the majority of these visitors were mamas and papas and aunts and grandmamas chaperoning marriageable young women whom the dowager duchess thought might catch her son's eye and perhaps his heart.

"I cannot understand my very own son," the dowager confided in the ancient ear of the Earl of Monmouth one June afternoon as they wandered together through the gardens. "Julius is handsome and wealthy and a duke for goodness sake, and yet he is not married. You would think that some young woman would use her head and discover the path to my son's heart. But they never do. They never do. It is almost as though Julius has fallen under some spell, and all the flirts and frivolities of all the young ladies in all of England are doomed to failure should they once be focused upon my son. What can be wrong with the boy, Nathan? He is twenty-seven and long past the age to be setting up his nursery."

"Nothing wrong with Julius," Monmouth replied, holding the dowager's hand in his own. "Excellent young man, Julius. Any number of feminine hearts flutter the moment he glances at them. The only problem, I think, is that he does not glance at them often enough, or long enough, or with the correct attitude or something."

"Just so. That is precisely what I mean. What am I to do, Nathan? It is not as if I do not try," she added with a sigh. "I fill Bright with eligible young ladies year after year. Sixteen of Julius's friends have met their wives here during one summer event or another. And yet, Julius never seems to meet anyone who can steal his heart away."

"Well," the earl replied, putting her hand through the crook of his arm. "It might help, you know, if you could persuade the lad to come out of his library, Corinthia."

And that was just the thing. Apparently, the number of hours which The Emperor chose to spend perusing the volumes in his library each day was directly proportional to the number of eligible young ladies who filled the guest chambers at Bright. In fact, at the very moment that his mama complained mournfully to Lord Monmouth that she was like to be eighty before the boy chose himself a wife, The Emperor was just completing his fourth hour in the library for that particular day and was just paging through his fifth book when he stopped right in the middle of the volume and looked up and exclaimed aloud, "I never knew that!"

"Never knew what, Your Grace?" asked his butler, who was just passing by the library on his way to the servants' staircase.

"Neverby, look here!" cried The Emperor, rising from his chair and pointing with considerable interest at one of the pages before him as he strolled toward the doorway. "It is a poem by Lord Byron based, he claims, upon his visit to us last July."

"How wonderful that his lordship should write about us, Your Grace," Neverby smiled. Neverby was most fond of the duke and was always pleased when The Emperor was pleased.

"Very wonderful indeed," nodded Amber, "but he speaks here of our nightingale with a song 'like fairies weaving spells about one.' And he calls her 'goddess of goodness, more bright and shining than ever England knew she had.'

"I did not know that we had a nightingale, Neverby. To think that Bright should boast such an extraordinary thing. Only look here," he added, taking his butler by the elbow and drawing him into the library to stare down at three other volumes which lay open upon the library table. "I thought at first it was merely one of Lord Byron's flights of fancy, you know. But it cannot be, for our nightingale is mentioned in this guide book as the very best thing about Bright—which is quite something, you know, because Bright has the very best of everything. Yet it says right here that the nightingale is better than all.

"And this modern history says that 'though the excellence of the ancients has combined with the artistry of the moderns to create a wonder called Bright which will steal a visitor's heart away, it is Bright's sweet nightingale that will steal the visitor's soul.'

"And this one, Neverby, says that our nightingale is worth a trip from anywhere in the world and that once one hears it one will never wish to return to his homeland again. Is that not most remarkable, Neverby?" asked the duke, brushing a stray lock of his molasses-colored hair excitedly from his brow with one long, slim finger. "Did you know, Neverby, that we had a nightingale, and that it was such an extraordinary one as these books imply?"

"A nightingale? Well, of course we have a nightingale, Your Grace," mumbled Neverby, who could not for the life of him remember ever having seen or heard one anywhere about the grounds. "There are nightingales throughout all of England as I understand. They are quite common birds."

"They are?"

"Indeed, Your Grace. Doubtless you have seen one or two of them yourself and did not realize."

"I am not much for looking at birds."

"No, Your Grace."

"But our nightingale is not common, Neverby. Even Lord Byron says that it is not. Do you know where it is, Neverby?"

"Where what is, Your Grace?"

"Our nightingale."

"Well, well, I should imagine it is somewhere about."

"I wish to see it, Neverby," said the duke with a nod of his handsome head, his violet eyes glowing with enthusiasm. "I should like to see it, and to hear it sing as well. It does not seem proper that something so extraordinary as our nightingale should live here under my very nose and I have never seen nor heard it. Does it seem proper to you?"

"No, Your Grace," murmured Neverby, quite appalled at the excitement the very thought of this bird appeared to stir up in The Emperor's imagination.

"Well, and it does not seem proper to me either. I should like to see our nightingale, Neverby, very much. In fact, I should like to have our nightingale for tonight's entertainment. Is that possible, do you think? Yes, a charming idea. Mama will be thrilled with it. She will think I have brought it in to enchant the ladies. An excellent idea! I shall have our nightingale sing for us after dinner! Go and fetch the thing for me, Neverby."

"Yes, Your Grace," nodded Neverby and hurried off down the corridor. "Rotworms!" he muttered under his breath as he reached the door to the servants' staircase. "Rotworms!"

Rotworms was what Neverby said whenever he became upset. It meant nothing at all, but it always made him breathe a bit easier.

"As if I have not enough to do. Bright is filling with guests hour by hour. There is a sit-down dinner for thirty this very evening that I must oversee myself. But what must he require of me? To find him a nightingale to sing after dinner! What puts such things into his head? He ought to be out escorting one young lady or another about the gardens and attempting to decide which of the chicks he will take to wife, not sitting in that library all alone hiding from them all. Anyone would think His Grace had not the least notion why his mama invites so many people to Bright every summer. Oh, rotworms!"

Neverby had been born at Bright and gone into service there at the age of six. He had been a first footman when this very Duke of Amber was born. He had become the butler when first His Grace had gone off to Eton. He had served Julius Caesar Crofton for twenty-seven years, every year of the duke's life, and he was devoted to the man. And if The Emperor wanted this nightingale, then The Emperor would have it, just as he would have anything within Neverby's power to give him.

With quick steps, Neverby rushed through the plethora of chefs, assistant chefs, scullery maids, and pot boys in the huge kitchen and scurried out through the kitchen door into the kitchen gardens where the vegetables, like everything else at Bright, grew surrounded by flowers. With long strides he rushed toward the stables and was quite out of breath when he reached them, his face redder than the roses that climbed the outer walls of that ancient brick building. "Stillman," Neverby called to the stable master, who was just then supervising the unhitching of Lord

Dinerly's team. "Stillman, I must speak to you at once."

"Aye, Mr. Neverby, what be the matter?"

"There is a nightingale somewhere about Bright that sings remarkably well. Do you know of it?"

The burly stable master shook his head.

"But you must have heard of it, Stillman. Apparently visitors and guests have been writing about it in books. Lord Byron himself wrote of it in a poem."

"Niver heard of it," declared the stable master. "A bird, ain't it, a nightingale? Here, Jamie, watch that bigun. He be eating of your leathers."

"Yes, yes, a bird. A bird that sings."

"Ain't much fer birds. Horses I knows about, but birds? I kinnot think I could tell me a nightingale from a peregrine. Best ask old Monty, Neverby. Likely he knows. Birds live in gardens, don't they? Monty be head gard'ner. Likely he's seen the thing."

Neverby nodded and set off toward the gardener's cottage. "Monty," he called, sprinting through row upon row of gently ringing flowers. "Monty, I must speak with you."

The head gardener, who was just then setting a most wonderful lilac bush into the ground at the edge of his tiny home, ceased his efforts and listened most carefully to the duke's butler. Then he shook his head and shrugged. "Not in my gardens, Mr. Neverby. Never did hear no nightingale in my gardens. Be off in the meadow more likely, along the stream. Like meadows an' streams, I reckon. Nothin' but wrens and sparrows in my garden. Ought ta be asking the gamekeeper is what I think. Like as not he has seen the thing."

"Rotworms," muttered Neverby, turning back toward the main house. "Ask the gamekeeper. We have not had a gamekeeper since Lure died the year after little Fiona disappeared. Run wild our deer have since. Yes, and our hedgehogs, too. Monty is getting a sight too old. His mind is not near as nimble as it ought to be. How am I to ask the gamekeeper when there is none?"

Neverby stomped back in through the kitchen door and almost trampled one of the little scullery maids. "Rotworms!" he muttered. "Nightingales!"

"N-nightingales?" asked the girl, whose face was covered with grease, whose arms were filled with pots and pans, and whose name was Molly.

"Yes, nightingales. Away, girl. There is dinner for thirty on the horizon. Do not stand about doing nothing or you will lose your position, I promise you."

The little maid sighed and turned toward the scullery. "I wishes I could 'ear 'er sing right this verimost minit," she muttered. "I be so tired, and she always do make me feel so very much better."

"Wait!" shouted Neverby excitedly. "Who makes you feel better? Who do you wish to hear sing?"

"Well, the nightingale o' course. Ever' night on m'way home I stops and listens ta 'er. She do sing the most loverly songs. Sings ta m'pa, too, she do, especially when he is tired."

This longingly uttered phrase brought home to Mr. Neverby most abruptly the fact that Molly was not merely one of the scullery maids, but also the daughter of the duke's woodcutter and every night Molly walked home across the meadow and into the wood where her father's cottage lay. Did this nightingale live in the wood then? "Where is it?" he asked the girl hopefully.

"Where is what, Mr. Neverby?"

"The nightingale."

The little scullery maid stared at him as if he had lost his mind. "Where? Why she be upon one branch er another."

"In the wood?"

"O' course in the wood. Where else would a nightingale be at? At least, she is always in the wood at night when I go home to Pa."

"Can you lead me to it, Molly? It is most important, girl. It is so very important that if you lead me to this bird, I will see that you are given a place of your very own to stand this evening from where you can see His Grace and the guests eat. That would please you, would it not?"

"Aye," nodded Molly, quite overwhelmed with such condescension upon Mr. Neverby's part.

"Yes, and I shall raise you up in rank, as well, my dear. If you will help me to catch this nightingale and bring it here to sing for His Grace after dinner, I shall see you are made a—"

"A assistant ta the pastry chef?" asked Molly hopefully.

"Precisely so!"

"Well, but I don't know as anyone can *catch* her, Mr. Neverby. Ye do not mean ta 'urt her at all, do ye?"

"No, no, never. Simply to bring it here to sing for His Grace after dinner. He has set his heart upon hearing it."

"That be real nice. I reckon as she will come do ye ask her. I reckon as she would be pleased as punch ta sing fer our duke, 'specially since he 'as set 'is heart upon hearing 'er. Ye ought ta mention that first off."

Mention that The Emperor has set his heart upon hearing it first off? pondered Neverby, scratching at the bit of hair that remained upon the top of his head. I must not catch the thing? I must request it to come and sing for The Emperor, and it will be pleased to do so? What kind of nonsense is this? Rotworms!

# TWO

"You are going where?" asked the dowager duchess, glowering at Neverby and little Molly and the two footmen whom Neverby had ordered to join him.

"To the w-wood, Your Grace," stuttered Neverby uneasily, his toes pointing toward each other as he stood upon the cobbles amongst the flowers with Molly attempting to hide behind him.

"With thirty for dinner in a few hours? Neverby, how dare you to even think of such a thing? And why would you go to the woods for any reason? You have never been beyond this garden in your entire life! I cannot think what possesses you," she added with a hopeless glance at Lord Monmouth. "Has my entire household gone mad then? Am I to expect to see the tweenies riding horseback across the meadow next?"

"It is His Grace's wish, Your Grace," murmured Neverby.

"His Grace? My son sends you and this child and James and Charles off into the wood?"

"Yes, Your Grace."

"Great heavens! For what possible reason?"

"To fetch a nightingale to sing after dinner, Your Grace."

The dowager duchess's eyebrows rose high in surprise and disbelief. Her routinely stubborn jaw slackened and she tugged at her ear lobe convulsively, which she was wont to do whenever she became extremely confused and upset.

"His Grace says that if he does not have the nightingale, he will not come to dinner at all," Neverby offered nervously.

"Then you had best be off and hurry quickly back," suggested Lord Monmouth, who knew well what inner turmoil Her Grace's tugging upon her earlobe signaled. "Do not you think so, Corinthia? If it is His Grace's wish—"

"Y-yes, of course," nodded the dowager in confusion. "Go, Neverby. Hurry. Thirty to dinner at eight! Oh, Nathan," she sighed as the butler, the scullery maid and the two footmen rushed off down the cobbled path, "has my Julius turned lunatic? He has sent them off to capture a bird to sing after dinner? A bird? And if they do not return with it, he will not dine with his guests at all? I think I am going to faint. I know I am. I am going to faint dead away!" And the dowager began to wobble most unsteadily, forcing Lord Monmouth to place his arm supportively around her waist and to lead her to the very closest bench where he sat her down and allowed her to rest her suddenly aching head upon his broad but ancient shoulder.

With little Molly in the lead, the nightingale hunters reached, after a time, the most remote boundary of the flower gardens and, looking around them with great interest because Neverby and the footmen had never been so very far from the house before, they stepped cautiously into the meadow. Far to their right the stream gurgled along its path.

"Oh my," exclaimed James, the first footman, "what a pleasant and relaxing sound. It is no wonder that His Grace wishes to have it."

Molly stared up at the tall, gangly fellow. Her eyes crinkled in laughter. "Do ye think that little gurgle be made by the nightingale? That be but the stream travelin' on its way ta the ocean. The stream do always sound that way, but ye can't be takin' it back to sing after dinner."

"Indeed," nodded Neverby, who had also thought the sound had been made by the nightingale, but did not wish to appear so unknowledgeable as the footman. "That is merely the stream, James. Do you not know the sound of a stream when you hear one?"

They continued on, the three men and the tiny girl, until they reached the middle of the meadow where the baaing of a sheep reached their ears and the three men came to an immediate halt.

"My, how unique and plaintive, certainly a bird that can produce such a sound as that is most special," declared the second footman. "It is not at all amazing that His Grace wishes to view this thing. It must be a most wonderful bird indeed to produce such a sound as that."

Neverby, amazed as well by the baaing, was about to nod in agreement, when little Holly informed them with a giggle that the baaing came from a creature called a sheep.

"It is nothing but a sheep, Charles," Neverby said, staring down his very superior nose at the fellow. "Do you not know a sheep when you hear one?"

"I have never before heard a sheep," the footman replied honestly, his face reddening.

"Well, that is precisely what they sound like,"

Neverby explained as though he had actually heard one before.

"Come on," urged Molly. "We 'ave got a bit ta go yet, an' we must git back in time fer servin' dinner." She led them all the way across the meadow to the very edge of the wood in which she and her father lived, and paused to peer into the trees.

Around them a chorus of tree frogs began to croak, but before any of the men could open their mouths, Molly declared that the frogs were not the nightingale either and that the nightingale was likely flitting from tree to tree inside the wood itself. With chin high, she stepped among the trees, the butler and the two footmen following most cautiously, not one of them ever having been among the trees before, and all of them a bit fearful of the shadowy, dense wood.

They walked in single file, all heads but Molly's turning about as though upon a swivel and looking up and looking down and peering between the pines and oaks and elms to see what might be peering back at them from the depths of the woods. And then, without the least warning, Molly stopped. Mr. Neverby, busily searching the branches above him at the time, did not notice and walked smack into her, knocking the poor child to the ground. Just as he was reaching down to help her up, James the first footman, who was positive that he was seeing the most frightening red eyes staring hungrily out at him from behind an ancient oak, collided with Mr. Neverby's back and sent the butler sprawling. Charles, the second footman, worriedly glancing over his shoulder, noticed nothing in front of him at all and ka-thumped into James, adding him to the pile of humanity upon the ground.

"Well, for goodness sake," Charles declared, "why

is everyone down there?" And being a kindly and thoughtful man, he immediately helped them all to rise. Just as he lifted little Molly to her feet, the most beautiful sound began to flow about them. As sweet and perfect as the pudding on Christmas, it held them immobile in fascination and literally stole their breath away.

"That be the nightingale," grinned Molly, peering up into the trees about them. "There she be," she cried, pointing to a small branch in the closest of the elms. "G'af'ernoon to ye, Miss Nightingale. We 'ave come by order of the duke hisself. Mr. Neverby do 'ave somethin' ta ask ye. Go on," urged Molly. "Ask 'er. An' say it right like I told ye."

Neverby, thoroughly overcome by the sweetness of the nightingale's song, nevertheless pulled himself together like the competent butler he was, and said quite as if he did believe that there was nothing at all batty about a person speaking to a nightingale, "Good afternoon. I have the pleasure to say that the Duke of Amber has thirty guests to dinner and requests your presence this very evening to sing for them afterward. He very much looks forward to hearing you himself, and he hopes that you will accept his invitation." Actually, now that it had ceased to sing and was cocking its head one way and then the other upon the limb above his head, Neverby took note that it was truly a drab bird, brown and gray and not at all remarkable to gaze upon, and he did wonder whether or not His Grace would be pleased with it.

"The Emperor invites me to Bright? Right into the house?" asked the bird.

"Humph?" gasped Neverby, quite taken aback to hear the nightingale speak. Rotworms! he thought to calm himself. Rotworms! What sort of nonsense is this? Surely there is someone behind the elm making jest of me. With slow steps Neverby walked forward, circled the tree, and then came back to stand between Molly and the footmen. No one there. No one anywhere about but themselves and the bird.

"I should be most happy to sing for The Emperor," continued the nightingale. "What time must I appear?"

"Come with us now and we will show you the way," offered James, nervously tugging at the long ringlets of his powdered wig. "You may even ride upon my shoulder if you like."

"No, I shall come all on my own," replied the nightingale. "Only say what time I am to arrive and leave the drawing room window open for me. With thirty guests His Grace will doubtless wish me to entertain in the long drawing room, will he not?"

"Precisely so," Neverby responded. "Dinner is at eight. I expect you ought to come at ten. That will put you in the room before the ladies withdraw."

"I shall be prompt," nodded the little bird. "Have you a perch for me to sit upon?"

"I will make you one," Charles offered affably.

"No, you will not," protested James. "You will be serving at dinner with all the rest of us."

"I will make it before dinner," Charles responded. "It ain't hard to make a perch."

"If dinner is at eight, you ought to be off. It is a very long walk back to Bright," the nightingale suggested, and then she trilled the loveliest scale and flapped her wings and flew deeper into the wood.

\* \* \*

Julius Caesar Crofton paced his library in measured strides, his violet eyes bright with anticipation. For the first time since his mama's guests had begun to arrive, he looked forward to dinner and to the entertainment afterward. "It will be the most remarkable thing," he told himself. "People will remark upon it for years to come. 'Only think,' they will say, 'we were present at Bright the very evening that the nightingale sang.' And no one will even think to gain my attention or expect me to sit beside them or engage them in any sort of conversation or flirtation. Certainly not. Not while this exceptional bird is singing." And then he smiled to himself.

No matter what anyone might think, at the best of times it was difficult to be the Duke of Amber. He had always to be polite and cordial and condescending. He had always to be careful not to overstep himself in the presence of those less fortunate than he. He was expected to keep a rein upon his power so as not to offend and he must always look after his lands and his fortune. Yes, and he must always appear courageous and noble and loyal to boot.

But in the worst of times being the Duke of Amber was impossible. And summers, since his coming of age, had become the worst of times. Every spring he managed to tread his way lightly through the Season in London, avoiding the lures young ladies in search of title and fortune tossed out to him, and balancing elegantly upon the fine line between sociability and eligibility, but every summer he came near to having an apoplexy as his mama filled Bright with every marriageable young lady she could find. Really, it was the outside of enough the way she flung the girls at him summer after summer after summer!

In that first summer of his coming of age, he had actually believed in love. And with hope in his heart that at twenty-one he would at last discover the mysteries of the poets' pens, he had attempted to please them all—his mama and the young ladies and the young ladies' chaperons—but he had learned quickly that it could not be done. The moment he would take one miss riding, the others would fall into despair. Whenever he achieved an interesting conversation with Lady So-and-So, Lady Such-and-Such burst into tears and rushed from the room. The sheer tension of it all had had him tugging at his earlobe every five minutes, much in the manner of his mama when she was discomposed. And so, splat in the middle of that first summer, he had given up in despair—given up on young ladies and pleasing his mama and even love, which he was beginning to believe did not truly exist anyway—and he had gone to drown himself in his books, where he had discovered the most amazing thing! No self-respecting young lady, apparently, ever set foot in a gentleman's library. He had made practical use of that knowledge ever since.

Though Fiona used to come into my library, he thought to himself sadly, remembering his childhood friend. *Fiona was almost as fond of perusing the volumes upon these shelves as I am myself. Still, Fiona is gone now, and there is no use at all in thinking about her. She will never come back to me.*

Bringing his pacing to a halt before the library window, the duke stared out into his gardens and listened to the soft chiming of the bells. He ran his fingers through his hair and nibbled upon his lower lip. "Where did you go, Fiona?" he whispered quietly. "Why did you leave me? Who was it took you away?"

He had searched for the answers to those questions for years, just as he had searched hopefully for Fiona, but there were no answers to be had, it seemed, and Fiona was not to be found. One summer's day, shortly before sunset, Fiona Lure had kissed him upon the cheek and raced away to the gamekeeper's cottage at the westernmost edge of the wood, and the following day she had not reappeared. She had not reappeared ever again. Her papa claimed that the gypsies had got her, but the duke highly doubted that. Gypsies, indeed. Even at sixteen the duke knew that gypsies did not go about stealing the twelve-year-old daughters of virtually penniless gamekeepers. Where was the profit in that enterprise?

"Fiona, where did you go?" he whispered again, his heart aching as it always did when he thought of her freckled little nose and smiling eyes. "Your papa is long dead, and I am besieged by ladies intent upon driving me mad. Why do you not come home and keep me from going mad? I would give all of Bright, give everything I have in all the world, if only it would bring you back to me."

And then the duke noticed the little parade of nightingale hunters marching toward the house along the cobbled paths through the gardens. He smiled softly. "At least I will not be besieged by mama's young ladies this evening," he murmured. "Unless they have not got the bird. But they will have it. Neverby would not return without it. I am certain he would not. Still, I do not see any of them carrying a cage with a bird in it."

In a matter of five minutes or so, Neverby appeared before the duke and bowed quite elegantly.

"Well, where is it, Neverby? Never say you could not find the thing."

"We found it most easily, Your Grace. Little Molly, one of the scullery maids, led us straight to it."

"And?"

"And?" asked Neverby, the least bit shaken by the way in which The Emperor cocked his left eyebrow.

"And did you catch it, Neverby? I do not see you holding anything in your hand. Where have you put it? I should like beyond anything to see the bird."

"Well, ah, you cannot see it at the moment, Your Grace."

"Why not?"

"Because she—it—is not here."

"Not here? You did not catch it then," sighed Amber, imagining how his dinner would feel rumbling about in his stomach as he attempted to entertain the plethora of young ladies his mama had invited while all the chaperons looked on.

"No, no, did not catch it. No need to catch it. It—she—it—it is a she, Your Grace. I think we must call it she. She will be here at ten o'clock on the dot. Charles is making a perch for her to sit upon even as we speak."

"*She* will be here at ten o'clock on the dot? How in the devil do you know?"

"Because I invited her and she agreed to come."

The Duke of Amber stared at his butler as if the man's cupboard were filled to the brim with chipped teacups. "You *invited* her, Neverby? You *invited* a bird? And you imagine that she agreed to come?"

"No, Your Grace. I invited her and she *did* agree to come."

"How do you know? Did she nod at you or some

such and you took that to have some meaning? Birds do nod all the time, Neverby. I do not know much at all about them, but I do know that. They are forever bobbing their heads up and down."

"She *said* she would come, Your Grace. At ten o'clock. I am to leave the window of the long drawing room open for her."

"Oh," nodded the duke, placatingly. "Yes. She *said* she would come. Well, that was most condescending of her, Neverby, considering she is so very famous and all. Would you—would you care to sit down for a while? It is quite hot outside, is it not? You ought to sit down for a while and just—you know—rest."

"I am not batty and I do not require a rest!" exclaimed Neverby in no uncertain terms. "The nightingale spoke to us. I vow she did, and she sang for us, too. And it was the most beautiful sound I have ever heard. And she will be here at ten o'clock to sing for you and your guests after dinner. I cannot help it, Your Grace, if it all seems a bit odd. It is odd. Rotworms! It is impossible! But it is true all the same!"

# THREE

Lady Elizabeth, the daughter of the Duke of Haarin-shire—due as much to the fact that the dowager duch-ess was quite taken with her as to her rank—sat on Amber's right at dinner. Eighteen, with golden curls and wide blue eyes, lips formed in a perfect Cupid's bow and the most engaging dimples in both cheeks, Lady Elizabeth knew herself to be the most beautiful and most eligible of the present contenders for the post of Amber's bride. A profoundly calculating young lady, she had spent the day investigating Bright and toting up in her mind what sort of fortune the fal-derols and furnishings of the place represented. She had noted every portrait, every painting, every chair and every carpet, each jeweled hilt upon display, each knickknack, each bevelled mirror. She had entered every room—except the library—and had put a price upon all she saw, and by dinner time her lovely eyes were wide with wonder and disbelief.

Why, he must be worth twenty times more than Papa, she thought, gazing coyly up at Amber from be-neath thickly lashed lids. Possibly even thirty times more. No wonder Mama was so determined we should accept the dowager's invitation. I do wish Papa had come with us to Bright. It would be most expedient to have Papa upon the scene so that His Grace may offer for me immediately he decides to do so, and not be made to write to Papa in London and wait about for his answer. Or perhaps His Grace will speak to Mama and she will give him permission to press his suit? No, Papa would not think to give Mama such power as that.

"Do you not care for venison, Lady Elizabeth?" ventured the duke, who had just completed carving the haunch that had been set before him.

"No, Your Grace. I am not one for venison. I always envision the buck with his magnificent rack bounding through the forest, and so I quite lose my appetite when venison is set before me."

"You will have some of the roast pig then, or a bit of the carp? You cannot possibly imagine a carp with a magnificent rack bounding through the forest."

Lady Elizabeth smiled. "Perhaps," she said, thinking to impress this handsome and exceedingly wealthy nobleman with her uniqueness, "I will take just a bit of the marrow pudding."

With a quick grin for little Molly who, as promised, had been given a place to stand and watch the dinner just beside the cherrywood sideboard, and a nod of his head at the first footman, the duke sent James down to the foot of the table to fetch the pudding for her. Marrow pudding! It was the one thing in the world that the duke truly detested, and his gorge rose as he saw it make its way onto her plate.

"Your father does not join us?" Amber observed after a long moment in which he fought his stomach into submission and refused to look at the marrow pudding even from the corner of his eye.

"He cannot. He must remain in London yet a fortnight."

"That is too bad, really. I should like to have had his opinion upon the odd fluctuations in the Funds of late. You are not at all interested in the Funds, I expect?"

Lady Elizabeth blinked up at him in the most bewitching fashion. Her Cupid's bow lips parted. She provided him on the instant with the most thorough appraisal of the Funds, why they were acting as they were, and a well-considered opinion of what might well be the outcome. "You are shocked, Your Grace," she added with a flirtatious batting of her eyelashes. "Young ladies are not expected to know anything at all about such things, I know. But I am quite fond of watching the Funds rise and fall."

Watching them rise and fall indeed, Amber thought, smiling his most sociable smile at her. She knows as much about the Funds as Haarinshire. No doubt learned the value of a pence at his knee at the age of six months. "You are an exceptional young lady," he said aloud. "I am quite stunned, but happily so. And what else do you enjoy, aside from watching the Funds?"

Elizabeth knew the perfect answer to this, for her mama had coached her all the way to Bright upon his grace's likes and dislikes. "I fear to admit it," she replied shyly, "but I am most fond of books. I love to sit in Papa's library from dawn to dusk and open one volume after another to see what they might contain. I have a passion for books."

"You do?"

"Indeed, Your Grace.

"You like to sit about in libraries?"

"Just so, Your Grace."

"Even when the sun is shining and there are an infinite number of enjoyable things to do outside?"

"Yes, Your Grace."

"Well, you are only the second young lady I have ever known who had such a preference as that, let me tell you."

"I do so hope to have the opportunity to view Bright's library," Lady Elizabeth said in a sultry little murmur. "I have heard it is positively magnificent."

The third course arrived and The Emperor politely switched his attention from Lady Elizabeth on his right, to the young lady on his left, who happened to be his cousin, Margaret.

"Do not bother with me, Julius," she adjured him. "I shall not feel at all slighted if you wish to continue your conversation with Lady Elizabeth."

"No, but I do not wish to continue my conversation with Lady Elizabeth, Margaret. Besides, it would be most improper of me to ignore you. You know it would."

"Balderdash. Your mama set me here just so that you *could* ignore me and get to know Lady Elizabeth better."

"Did she?"

"Yes, and do not look at me with such innocent surprise. You know perfectly well that I am not out to catch you for a husband, and that Lady Elizabeth and all the rest of the young ladies at this table are. Julius, you are driving your mama to distraction," she added with a grin. "Even now she is tugging viciously at her earlobe because she sees that you are wasting a precious opportunity by speaking to me."

"Rot," chuckled The Emperor. "Mama cannot possibly see me. The centerpiece is too high and too wide. What is she doing, standing upon her chair?"

"She can very easily see me, and see that I am engaged in conversation with the gentleman on my right and not the gentleman on my left. And the gentleman upon my right, Julius, is you."

"Oh. Well, I expect it is all Mama's fault if she tugs herself into some sort of fit. She is the one who taught me proper etiquette, and proper etiquette demands that I divide my conversation between you and Lady Elizabeth both. Besides, Margaret, I do not think that I like Lady Elizabeth."

"You do not? How can you know? You welcomed her when she arrived and then buried yourself in the library until you were forced to welcome some other young lady. You have not spent time with any of them, Julius. Nor have you spoken above a sentence apiece to them. Lady Elizabeth might well turn out to be the young lady of your dreams."

"No."

"No?"

"I do not think so. The young lady of my dreams is not called Elizabeth, and her hair is not blonde nor her eyes blue."

"Oh, Julius." Margaret felt such sudden pity for him that she was forced to twist her napkin tightly about her hand to keep from shedding tears. "You are remembering Fiona, are you not?" she whispered. "But she was a child merely, and you little more than a child yourself. You cannot place your hopes upon a dream of childhood. Why, if Fiona were to come to you this very evening, you might well discover that you detest her now that she is grown." If she is grown, Margaret added in her mind, for she was nearly certain that

Fiona had not been taken by gypsies or anything of the kind, but had been killed by some criminal and buried without anyone being the wiser. "Besides which, Julius, you know Fiona would be most ineligible. She was the daughter of your gamekeeper, for goodness sake. Your mama would never have countenanced such a match."

"I did not say that the lady of my dreams was Fiona."

"No."

"You ought not assume, Margaret."

"No. You are perfectly correct. I ought not."

"Apparently the tablecloth is leaving, and the port and peaches and biscuits are arriving," His Grace observed quietly. "Mama is standing, Margaret. I see the top of her head."

"Do not allow the gentlemen to linger long, Julius. It is after ten o'clock already," urged Margaret, setting her napkin aside and rising with all of the other ladies to withdraw.

Corinthia, the Dowager Duchess of Amber, led the way down the corridor to the long drawing room, stepped across the threshold and clutched her hand-painted chicken skin fan to her bosom. "Oh my," she gasped quietly.

"Aunt Corinthia, what is it?" asked Margaret, hurrying to her. "Why do you pause and stare so?"

"My son has lost his mind," murmured the dowager sadly. "Nathan attempted to convince me it could not be so, but there is the proof of it right before my eyes," and she pointed with one finger toward a tiny bird who sat upon a rough-hewn oaken perch beyond the pianoforte.

"Oh, what a funny little bird!" exclaimed Lady Elizabeth, looking over the dowager's shoulder.

"We shall just ignore it, Aunt Corinthia," whispered Margaret in the dowager's ear. "Come, we cannot keep all the ladies standing about in the corridor. We shall just not look at the thing if it offends you so."

"No, no, it does not offend me," protested the dowager, allowing Margaret to whisk her into the room and seat her upon the silk-covered sofa at the opposite end of the chamber. From there the duke's mama could not see the bird. She could not so much as make out the pianoforte without squinting up her eyes in the most abominable fashion. "He means to have it sing for us," the dowager confided in Margaret's ear while tugging violently at her own. "It is to be our after-dinner entertainment. Oh, Margaret, dearest, my Julius has popped his cork!"

"The duke means it to be our after-dinner entertainment," hissed Miss Antoinette Falsworth, who had had the excellent luck to stand just behind the dowager and overhear her words. "Our after-dinner entertainment," she repeated as Lady Angela Davenport leaned forward to better catch what she had said.

"I am mishearing you, dearest. You cannot have said that His Grace intends for that bird to be our after-dinner entertainment?"

"No, it is a jest," declared Lady Elizabeth when her mama carried to her the word of the bird's purpose. "The duke has set that rumor about himself to have a bit of fun with us."

Lady Wharton, a sparkle in her aging eyes as her very nervous granddaughter relayed the purpose of the bird into her ear, laughed. "His Grace is perpetrating a jest upon the lot of us, Carola. You must not be so very fearful of him, my dear. I promise you that Julius Caesar Crofton is not a madman nor an ogre, and I am quite certain that when he stops to speak with you, you will discover that he possesses just ordinary teeth like anyone else, and not fangs, my dear!"

"Well, you know what it means," murmured the dazzling, dark-haired Miss Templeton-Smith, when word of it reached her.

"No, what?" asked her younger sister.

"That the duke is as queer as Dick's hatband."

"Oh, it does not," protested Miss Elena Templeton-Smith. "Most likely it means that he is fond of birds and nothing more."

Word of The Emperor's intentions buzzed through the chamber like a swarm of bees as young ladies and elderly ladies alike pondered over the significance of the drab, quiet little bird at the far end of the chamber, and wondered what on earth His Grace had in mind to suggest that *it* would entertain them. In the end, the chamber became equally divided between those who believed His Grace to be perpetrating a great hoax upon the entire house party and those who thought that the duke had taken a tumble going over rough ground and had arisen short a sheet.

Those who thought The Emperor suddenly short a sheet—including his own mama—saw more proof for their conclusion when the gentlemen arrived fifteen minutes later with the duke in the lead holding the hand of a little scullery maid.

When all of the household servants, including the fireboys and the potboys entered upon the gentlemen's heels and went to stand quietly along the drawing room walls, lifted eyebrows and whispers behind fans emphasized that those ladies who sided with the duke's mama may have been right all along.

"Is everyone here, do you think, Molly?" asked the duke, kneeling down beside the little girl.

"Ever' one I knows is here, Yer Grace."

"Good. Everyone I know is here as well. Take Charles then, and bring our nightingale to the center of the room. Can you do that, my girl?"

"Oh, yes, Yer Grace, but you must tell Mr. Charles to help me, becuz he wont be takin' orders from no scullery maid."

"But you are no longer a scullery maid, I hear. Neverby tells me you are now an assistant pastry chef."

"I is?" cried Molly joyfully. "Now? Right now?"

"The very moment that you and Charles bring my nightingale forward."

Molly scurried away, grabbed the second footman by the hand and tugged him off toward the pianoforte. With a bit of bumping and amongst a great deal of whispering, Charles carried the perch he had made to the middle of the long drawing room while Molly followed with the nightingale perched upon her finger.

When at last the perch was in position and the bird back upon it, when the amazed and amused and astounded whispers died and all of the gentlemen and ladies had found a place to sit or stand comfortably, the Duke of Amber strolled to the center of the chamber, bowed before the nightingale, and said quite properly, "Welcome, Miss Nightingale, to my home. I am most pleased to have you here."

The nightingale of course, as he had known it would, simply cocked her head at him and ruffled her feathers and did not speak. Why Neverby vowed it had spoken, the duke could not guess, but it made not the least difference to him. The nightingale, which had been called the very best thing in all of Bright, was before him at last and he was eager to hear her sing.

"Will you honor us with a song, my dear?" he asked, and the nightingale nodded as nightingales often do.

"Well then, I thank you, and I will take myself off and leave the floor to you."

At that moment, everyone in the chamber was upon the verge of whispering about the poor dear duke and what might be done for him, if anything might—except, of course, Molly and James and Charles and Neverby, who quite understood that the nightingale must be properly addressed. But then, before a word could actually be spoken, the drab little bird's throat rippled and pulsed and the nightingale began to sing. She sang of love and of life, of joy and of sorrow; she sang all of the songs of all of the hearts of all of the people in the tiny Empire of Amber. Like liquid gold her songs flowed through the drawing room, silencing the whispers before they began and weaving a fairies' web of wonder around the ladies and the gentlemen, the upper servants and the lower servants, and especially around the duke himself.

No one dared to move, to speak, to breathe as the nightingale sang—except The Emperor. Having taken a seat upon the sofa beside his mama, in the midst of the glorious singing, he raised one slender hand to brush at sudden tears that coursed one after the other down his closely shaved cheeks. He attempted to stop them from flowing, but he could not. The song of the nightingale filled his heart to overflowing with a mixture of such sweetness and such sadness, such goodness and such loss, that his tears shone like jewels upon his kind and handsome face and would not be held back no matter how hard he tried.

The nightingale sang and sang far into the night. And the people all remained precisely where they were—ladies, gentlemen, and servants alike sat and stood and leaned precisely where they had when first she began, but their hearts and their souls sailed off on gossamer wings to places they had never seen and might well never see again. When at last the nightingale ceased to sing, The Emperor, still swiping at his tears, arose and went to her. "You are indeed the very best thing in all of Bright," he whispered, stroking the soft feathers of her breast. "I wish you to remain with me forever."

# FOUR

In the quiet of his own chambers late that night, the Duke of Amber urged the nightingale—whom he had caused to have brought up to him—from off her perch and up upon his finger and he stroked her softly and with a great deal of tenderness. "I have only cried once before in all my life," he murmured to her. "I was only sixteen then, when Fiona disappeared. A boy of sixteen may cry, I think, when his heart is broken."

"There is no shame in tears," replied the nightingale.

Julius Caesar Crofton's wide violet eyes opened even wider, and he stared at the bird in wonder.

"The tears of the Duke of Amber, like rare and exotic jewels, are priceless," the nightingale said. "You have honored me this night beyond your ability to know."

"You—you *do* speak!"

"Yes. Did you not realize? You sent your invitation to me so politely that I was certain you knew that I was no common bird."

"No, yes, of course I knew that you were by no means common, but I did not know that you—that you could—speak. Well, but that is not true either. Neverby did mention it, but I did not believe him. I thought he had lost his mind."

"And yet you honored him tonight by allowing him to attend you in the drawing room. You honored all of your servants this night. And you honored little Molly most of all just by taking her hand into your own."

"I shall keep you with me always," declared Amber emphatically. "I shall have a tiny jeweled collar made for you to wear about your throat, and I shall buy a golden cage for you to live in with a golden swing upon which you may perch and sing to your heart's content, and no cat shall ever find you. No, nor no dog or ferret or any other predator. You shall be warm and well-fed and safe from fear for all your life."

The nightingale cocked her drab head at The Emperor in the most beguiling way, and his heart swelled within him.

"I do not wish such honors as that," she said then. "I have a beautiful wood as green as emeralds in which to live, and any number of branches and twigs upon which to perch. When I am cold, I find my own shelter, and when I am hungry, I find my own food. And if there are predators, I do not live in such fear of them that I would trade my freedom to be safe. To be confined within this house would chafe my soul, Your Grace, just as sorely as your jeweled collar would chafe my neck."

"But you cannot leave me," protested the duke.

"I shall remain in this house for as long as you desire me," the nightingale replied, "but only if you always leave a window open in whatever room I am to reside. For then I may fly in and out as I please, Your Grace."

"I will do it," nodded Amber.

"Then I will never leave you. I shall be with you always."

With this promise, the little bird flew from His Grace's finger and alighted upon the perch which the second footman had made for her. Smiling a most intriguing birdlike smile, she began to fluff and preen herself and settle in to sleep.

The duke's valet scratched upon the chamber door and entered to prepare His Grace for bed. He spoke of the nightingale's beautiful song as he helped the duke out of his form-fitting blue velvet jacket. He praised the delicacy and sweetness of the notes as he removed His Grace's shoes. He spoke with gratitude of His Grace's great condescension toward his staff for allowing them to hear the nightingale sing, as he untied the ties of His Grace's breeches. "Surely that little bird is the very best thing in all of Bright," the valet murmured, as he helped Amber to don his nightshirt and step up into the great four-poster bed. "Good night, Your Grace. May your dreams be pleasant ones."

"Oh, Farthingale, I almost forgot!" exclaimed the duke. "Open my window a bit, will you?"

"Open your window? But the night air, Your Grace. It is known to be treacherous. Surely you do not wish—"

"I wish to have my window open," insisted Amber. "You need not fling it wide, Farthingale. Just a bit will do. Far enough for a nightingale to fit through it will be fine."

The valet did as he was requested, but frowned worriedly to himself as he left the chamber. Everyone knew that the night air was treacherous. Why, His Grace had never in his life wished his window to be

open to the night. Farthingale pondered over whether
he ought to report this newly acquired eccentricity to
His Grace's mama, but then he thought not. Her
Grace had undergone a most strenuous evening, or
so the kitchen gossip said, and he did not wish to dis-
turb her more with such unsettling news.

"Why can you talk?" asked Amber, staring at the
little bird in the light of the candle beside his bed.
"Do all nightingales speak?"

"No, Your Grace, all nightingales do not speak. I
am an enchanted nightingale."

"Enchanted? By whom?"

"By the faeries, Your Grace. The ones who live in
the verimost bottom of your gardens."

"There are faeries in my gardens?"

"Oh, yes, Your Grace, an entire colony of them, and
they were so very kind as to grant me my dearest wish."

"To speak."

"No, to sing the most beautiful songs in all the world
and to fly up into the moonlit sky on wings as soft as
velvet and to bring you, Your Grace, the greatest joy
that one such as I may bring. Now put out your candle
and go to sleep, do," she added, tucking her little head
beneath a wing. "I have had a most amazing day, and
I am exhausted."

The Emperor raised himself upon his elbow and
leaned over and snuffed the candle, then he settled
himself down upon the feather mattress. She has had
an amazing day? he thought, yawning. I have a nightingale in my chamber who speaks the King's English
and tells me that there is a colony of faeries in the
bottom of my gardens who grant wishes, and the bird
thinks that *she* has had an amazing day?

\* \* \*

From that evening forward the house party at Bright revolved as much around the nightingale as it did around the Duke of Amber. Every evening after dinner the bird sang, and everyone present when it sang became bewitched by its song. And the most bewitched of all was clearly The Emperor, himself.

The possibilities presented by this predilection of the duke for the nightingale were not lost upon the mamas and the papas, the aunts and the grandmothers, who had escorted their most marriageable young ladies into the tiny Empire of Amber to charm its handsome and wealthy ruler into marriage. The two Templeton-Smith sisters spent entire mornings before the looking glass in their dressing room with their papa beside them, learning first to whistle and second to actually whistle a tune. Lady Angela Davenport at her mama's instigation began to nod most curiously whenever the duke spoke to her and to cock her head from side to side at him in the most birdlike manner, practically twittering her responses to his sallies. And Miss Antoinette Falsworth, with her Aunt Beatrice's help, kept a glass of water always beside her, and before she spoke, she would take a sip and then attempt to gurgle out her comments in vague imitation of the nightingale's pulsating, throbbing notes.

Rotworms! thought Neverby whenever he set tea before the young ladies, or opened the door to them, or poured their wine at dinner, they are all of them moon-mad. I have never seen such nonsense in all my life. How His Grace can keep a straight face in the presence of such silliness I cannot conceive.

Actually, His Grace could not keep a straight face for very long. Where once he had gone to his library to hide away from his guests as long as was politely possible and to lose himself in his books until he knew he must return into their presence, now he would abruptly excuse himself—sometimes in the very middle of a conversation—and dash willy-nilly from wherever he happened to be into the library, closing the door with a definite ka-chunk behind him, and then he would burst into the most gleeful whoops, sometimes laughing with such hilarity that he found himself gasping for breath and forced to sit down and put his head between his knees to recover from it.

"You ought to be ashamed," Margaret giggled one afternoon, having followed directly upon his heels to discover what it was he did when he dashed off right in the midst of things.

"I—I—know," gasped The Emperor, "but I c-cannot help myself. Did—did you—s–see the manner in which Miss Bonner was r-running about?"

"She had to run about, Julius. We were playing blindman's buff, and she was the blindman."

"Yes, but she had that cloth tied 'round her eyes and she was flapping her arms as though she were some huge, demented chicken. I thought I should choke on my laughter if I did not get away immediately."

"She d-did look like a d-demented chicken," giggled Margaret, "but she certainly did n-not intend it as s-such."

"No, I know," the duke replied, his laughter softening. "She had every intention of imitating a nightingale with the gr-graceful move-move-ment of her w-w-wings!" and he was off again, slapping his hands upon the chair arms and chortling.

"Shame, Julius!" Margaret attempted to reprimand

her cousin, but it carried not the least sting because she was laughing much too heartily at the time.

"Are you not going to do anything at all to attract the man, Elizabeth?" asked the Duchess of Haarinshire quietly, as she joined her daughter in her bedchamber. "Do you not like him at all then?"

"Oh, I like him quite well, Mama. But I am not about to make a fool of myself by going about pretending somehow to be a nightingale. Do not say that you wish to see me strolling through the gardens whistling like the Templeton-Smith sisters."

"No, I think that most improper behavior in a young lady. But His Grace is so inordinately fond of that nightingale, you know. Perhaps if you were to befriend the thing and teach it to eat from your hand. That would be exceptional, I think."

"Mama, he keeps the bird in his bedchamber!"

"Oh? Oh! Well, of course you cannot teach it to eat from your hand if you must go into his bedchamber to do it!"

"No. But I have the most excellent idea."

"You have?"

"Indeed. Since His Grace is so fond of feathers, I have every intention of providing him with some—and much finer feathers than that drab little bird possesses. Come, Mama, we are going to the village."

"Now, Elizabeth?"

"This very moment."

The tiny haberdasher in the village of Minor-Glistening-on-the-Stream had never seen such a fine young lady as Elizabeth. He knew on the instant that she was Quality and so had come from Bright, and being quite dependent upon the occupants of Bright for most of his business, as were all the other merchants in that part of the world, he was moved to treat Lady Elizabeth and her mama with every deference. He listened with great interest to Lady Elizabeth's demands and when she had finished, he smiled and bowed his way out of the showroom to the very back of the shop. He took his little ladder and climbed to the very top shelf, tugged from the rear of it a rather battered bandbox, and scurried back down the ladder.

"This will be precisely the thing," he said, as he reentered the showroom. And opening the box, he plucked from it the most amazing hat which he set carefully upon Lady Elizabeth's shining golden curls. "Charming," he said. "Remarkable. Exquisite."

"It is perfect!" exclaimed Lady Elizabeth, staring at herself in the looking glass, tilting her head first one way and then the other. "Is it not perfect, Mama?"

"It is, ah, quite out of the ordinary," her mama responded slowly. "Elizabeth, are you certain that you wish to—"

"Oh, yes, Mama," interrupted that young lady. "I am very certain. It is just the thing, do not you see? One look and His Grace will be overwhelmed."

His Grace *was* overwhelmed. Completely bowled over in fact. All the members of the house party were having tea in the imitation Grecian temple in the middle of the gardens, when Lady Elizabeth returned. As she swept along the cobbled path toward them, the red and green and blue and black feathers of which her enormous hat was made rippled and wobbled in the wind. The flowers chimed around her. Her mama raced along behind. Amber came near to being struck dumb. His mouth fell open; his eyes stared; his hand paused with a cherry tart halfway to his lips.

"We are so frightfully sorry to be late," Lady Elizabeth announced as she glided up the steps into the temple, "but Mama did discover that she had forgotten to pack her vinaigrette and so we were forced to run off to the village to purchase a bottle. She cannot be without her vinaigrette, you know. One never knows when it may be required."

"J—just so," the duke replied, sounding somewhat smothered, his wide violet eyes fastened upon the monstrous hat as he arose with the other gentlemen to greet them. "You l—look absolutely ch-ch-charming, my lady," he managed.

Margaret's eyes flashed at him and he strove manfully not to burst out into guffaws as she, devil that she was, bowed her head, opened her fan before her face and snickered down into it in such a way that not one person noticed except The Emperor.

Lady Angela Davenport cocked her dark head one way and then the other as His Grace escorted Lady Elizabeth and the Duchess of Haarinshire to a pair of white wicker chairs and served them tea and cakes with his own hands. Miss Antoinette Falsworth, upon seeing this distinction, took a long sip of tea and enviously gurgled how nice it was to have them come and join the fun. The Templeton-Smith sisters burst into nervous whistling the moment it looked as though His Grace might actually think to move his own chair next to Lady Elizabeth's, and Miss Diana Scott, who until this very moment had done nothing at all extraordinary, rose to her feet and began to hop about in the most alarming birdlike manner from one side of the temple to the other and back again twittering about these flowers beside the temple here and those flowers beside the temple there, until at last her papa, with a glare at her mama, rose and caught his daughter by the shoulders and took her back to her own seat.

The dowager duchess watched the entire scene aghast. "They are all of them quite out of control," she hissed in Lord Monmouth's ear. "Nathan, it is most appalling. What do they think they are doing?"

"They merely attempt to appear birdlike, m'dear," Lord Monmouth replied, giving her knee a gentle and reassuring pat.

"But why?"

"To impress your Julius."

"Oh, great heavens! Do they think that my son intends to marry a bird?"

"No, no, certainly not. Cease tugging upon your ear, Corinthia, and pass me a tart, eh? There is nothing to be upset about, m'dear. Youthful spirits merely. They see that Julius is enamored of the nightingale and hope to transfer his enchantment from the bird to themselves, but they cannot discover, I think, what it is about the bird that bewitches him so."

"Nonsense!" hissed Her Grace. "Anyone with a brain knows it is the bird's singing that enchants him, as it does all of us. And here they are flitting and hopping about and whistling and cocking their heads from side to side and gurgling of all things, and Elizabeth prancing about with near a ton of quail feathers on her head. Not a one of them has thought to sing."

"Not yet," chuckled Lord Monmouth. "But I fear that at any moment one of them will burst into an aria."

None of them did, however, for which the dowager

duchess and Lord Monmouth and any number of mamas and papas and aunts and grandmothers gave thanks. The tea party came off very nicely in the end. Except for dashing from the temple once—after he went to sit beside a perfectly lovely Miss Marianne Marfet and the girl actually peeped at him like a tiny chick—His Grace behaved with great politeness and decorum and singled out none of the girls by simply singling out them all.

Still, Lady Elizabeth's hat of feathers and the Duke of Amber's reaction to it had quite stirred the young ladies' souls and their imaginations as well, and the very next morning a parade of carriages drove from Bright into Minor-Gistening-on-the-Stream and a veritable plague of gentlewomanhood descended upon the shopkeepers in search of anything and everything that might be worn with or made of or made to bear feathers. The merchants of Minor-Glistening-on-the-Stream rejoiced. The tills of Minor-Glistening-on-the-Stream swelled with monies paid, and that very morning thirty pheasants, thirty-five roosters, and one ancient peacock gave up their splendid raiment all in the cause of luring The Emperor into the parson's mousetrap.

# FIVE

Each day the ladies strove to impress Amber with their beauty, their wit, their gracefulness, their innate abilities to mimic birdlike habits and attitudes, and various bits of feathered finery. But each evening, after the nightingale sang, His Grace went off to his chambers without having distinguished by his attentions one young lady above all the others.

"It is good, I think, that this nightingale has come," murmured the dowager duchess late one night, as she and Margaret held a comfortable coze in Margaret's chamber. "I feared for a time that my Julius had lost his mind, but that nightingale sings the most beautiful songs I have ever heard, and when the day is done and dinner over and all the games and entertainments of our own devising are finished, I long to hear it."

"And I," nodded Margaret. "And our guests as well. Even the gentlemen call for her."

"Even Nathan," the dowager agreed. "He says that the nightingale's songs nourish his very soul."

"Just so, Aunt Corinthia."

"Yes, and Julius has ceased to hide away in his library all day, have you noticed that? Ever since the nightingale arrived, he has been all that I could hope for in a host. Why, he has even gone with us to share an *al fresco* nuncheon at the ruins of Tybart Castle, which he has never done in all the summers since I have begun to invite young ladies here."

"He finds these particular young ladies amusing, Aunt Corinthia. He cannot begin to imagine what they will do next to imitate that bird, and I do believe that he wakes each morning in anticipation of what he will see and hear from that quarter."

"Well, that is something at least." The dowager, already in her night rail, with her ruffled lace cap perched rather sweetly upon her graying curls, began to fiddle nervously with the ribands upon her green silk robe. "Margaret," she asked, staring down at the ribands, "is it so very wrong of me to wish to see Julius married and beginning to start his family?"

"Well, of course it is not wrong of you," Margaret responded at once. "You are merely longing to know, Aunt Corinthia, that he will have an heir and that the title will pass on as expected. And you wish a grandchild or two to dandle upon your knee. And doubtless, you wish for a younger lady to attend to the household matters as well. Of course it is not wrong."

"I do think it is past time for me to withdraw," sighed the dowager. "I know that there are any number of titled ladies and even some untitled ones who oppose surrendering their authority to their daughters-in-law, but—but I am not one of them. I have been the sole person in charge of Bright since six months before Julius was born. I should so like to be shed of the responsibility and be free again."

"Free, perhaps, to become the Countess of Monmouth?" asked Margaret softly.

The dowager's eyes, which were as wide and as wonderful as her son's, looked up into Margaret's and bubbled with laughter. "Oh, you naughty child!"

"Yes, I am. But Aunt Corinthia, Lord Monmouth is madly in love with you. Anyone with eyes can see that."

"Except my son."

"Well, but perhaps Julius *does* see it."

"Then he would marry and set me free to do the same. I cannot simply walk off and abandon Julius, you know, Margaret. He has not the first idea how to go on when it comes to the servants and the household. Oh, he knows very well how to manage the estates and the Funds and what to plant and whether a pasture is to be put to sheep or cattle, but does he know how often mattresses are to be turned, or what must be used upon the carpeting to take out a stain, or exactly how many quarts of strawberries must be preserved for the winter? Never. I vow, I think the boy believes that the mattresses turn themselves whenever they desire to do so, that carpets all shed their skins and renew themselves overnight, and that strawberries come off the vines right in their own jars!"

Lady Elizabeth stared from her bedchamber window out into the gardens that surrounded Bright. The night was warm and fair and stars glittered in the heavens, while a soft breeze set the tiny bells upon the flowers to chiming, which lent a delightful sensation of peace to the darkness. In her white muslin nightgown, with her hair in papers, Lady Elizabeth knelt upon the window seat, her palms pressing upon the sill as she stuck her head out through the open lattice followed by her slim shoulders.

"Elizabeth!" hissed a voice from behind her. "What in heaven's name do you think you are doing? Come inside at once. You will fall and kill yourself."

"No, Mama, I will not," Lady Elizabeth sighed, gazing back over her shoulder. "It is merely that I hear him."

"Hear whom?" asked her mama, moving closer.

"His Grace, Mama. I hear him speaking, but I cannot quite make out his words."

"Elizabeth! That is eavesdropping!"

"Yes, I know," the young lady replied with a scowl as she pulled her shoulders and head back inside the window and turned to face her mother. "And if you do not cease to rattle on so, Mama, I shall never be able to make out what he says. His chambers are not so very far away, I think. Though I cannot tell in which direction they lie, for his voice tends to hover about on the breeze and one time comes from here and another from there."

"Elizabeth, close that window at once!"

"Absolutely not. How am I to know what His Grace thinks of me if I do not listen to him?"

"If you cannot make out what it is he says, how do you know he is speaking of you at all, Elizabeth?"

"Well, he must be, Mama. About whom else would he speak? Certainly not the Templeton-Smith sisters. I vow, Mama, if those girls do not cease to whistle at every opportunity afforded them, I shall sneak into their chambers one night and sew their lips together. The sound of their whistling does grate upon one's nerves so. And the very next time that Miss Scott insists upon prancing about in a manner which she considers to be birdlike, I shall toss a worm at her."

"No, you will not. You shall behave in a ladylike fashion no matter what the others may do. Now close the window, Elizabeth, and get to bed. It is very late and you do not wish to break your fast in your own chamber tomorrow morning. His Grace has been pre-sent at the breakfast table every morning at nine for the past week, and not one young lady has deigned to come down and join him. Why, when I was your age, I should never have thought to break my fast in bed. It is nothing but an entire morning of opportunities wasted."

Elizabeth's scowl lightened. She almost smiled as she pulled the lattice closed and latched the latch. "I forgot," she murmured. "I forgot about breakfast. No one else realizes that he breaks his fast at nine. Oh, Mama, I am so very happy that you discovered it."

"Yes, well, I could not help but discover it. I have been breakfasting with His Grace and Corinthia and Nathan for seven entire days now. His mama, of course, has always been an early riser. Why, when Corinthia and I were girls, we often were up and away by nine—to shop, or ride in the park with our grooms to accompany us. In London during the Season, of course. We came out together, Corinthia and I."

"Just so, Mama. I know. You have told me about your coming out any number of times. And now I have come out myself."

"Indeed. I feel quite ancient, to tell the truth," the Duchess of Haarinshire complained. "Any day now I think to gaze into my looking glass and discover an old woman staring back at me. I shall feel excessively sad when that day arrives."

Elizabeth began to say that her mama was already an old woman, but thought better of it. It would not do to have her mama angry with her—not now. "You make too much of it, Mama," she said instead. "It is because you have a grown son and daughter that you feel old. Everyone knows that you were but a child when you married Papa."

"That is true," nodded the duchess. "That is very true. And Corinthia was the same age when she chose to marry old Amber. I cannot think to this day why she did so. He was ancient, Elizabeth, and not at all handsome."

"Yes, Mama, but he was exceedingly wealthy, I think."

"No, no, Corinthia would not have married him for his money. Her papa was prodigiously wealthy himself. There must have been something about him that appealed to her. Perhaps it was his hair. He had the most enticing curls, old as he was. If I recall correctly, they were the exact color as his son's are now."

"Well, for whatever reason, she did choose to marry the Duke of Amber, Mama, and now I choose to marry their son."

"You do? You have decided?" asked the duchess, her eyes alight with glee. "Oh, Elizabeth, I am so very happy! He is a good deal more handsome than his papa ever was and he has Corinthia's eyes, and his form is perfection, I think."

"Yes, Mama," smiled Elizabeth, nodding. And he is thirty times more wealthy than any man in England, she added to herself. At least thirty times more wealthy. I shall be the envy of all my friends do I land this fat carp upon my little hook.

"You are driving your mother to Bedlam, and through her, me," declared the Earl of Monmouth, stretching his legs out before the fire in the duke's sitting room. "If you cannot like any of the young ladies she sets before you, Julius, then for gawd's sake go and find one for yourself."

The Duke of Amber, in shirtsleeves and dressing gown, offered the elderly lord a glass of brandy and sank into the matching wing chair beside him. "Perhaps I was never intended to be a married man, Nathan."

"Pah! You are the Duke of Amber. You have a title and estates to be kept in the line. You cannot do that without an heir, and you cannot have an heir if you are not married."

"That is not quite true," grinned Amber.

"No, but it is close enough. You are not thinking to pick an heir from among your cousins, Julius? Your father would roll over in his grave. Speaking of which, why have you a fire burning in here? It is exceedingly warm tonight."

The Duke of Amber laughed. "Fire and Papa come together in your mind? Think my father went in that direction, do you? Well, my fire is courtesy of a rascal named Tim."

"Tim?"

"Yes, Tim. He has just now reached his sixth year and has been promoted to fire boy."

"What was he before you promoted him?" asked Monmouth.

"He was the fetchit."

"The what?"

"The tyke that every one of the servants sent to fetch things they had forgotten or suddenly discovered they required. The fetchit. Do not tell me you have not such a position, Nathan?"

"All right," laughed the earl, "I will not tell you."

"At any rate, Tim has been practicing his fire lighting on this particular hearth so that when the cold weather comes at last, he will have got it down correctly. Neverby has apologized to me at least ten times this week for there being a fire in here. 'Rotworms!' he says, 'has that brat been at it again? I shall take a buggy whip to him.' Which he will not do, of course, because Tim is my housekeeper's—Mary Margaret's— son and Mary Margaret is Neverby's niece, and Neverby loves the girl and the lad with all his heart."

"So, behind Neverby's back, you encourage the lad to continue his practicing."

"I never said that—but yes, I do. I love to hear Neverby say rotworms. I always have loved to hear him say it."

"I am going to start crying rotworms myself if you do not settle down and find yourself a bride," laughed Monmouth.

"You are? Why?"

"Because, you madman, I mean to marry your mother, but she will not agree to it until you have a wife."

"Mama? You intend to marry Mama?"

"Do not look at me with such innocence, Julius. You have known for years that I mean to marry your mama."

"Yes," nodded the duke, pausing to sip his brandy. "And I intend that you shall do it, too, Nathan. I should very much like to see you and Mama marry. She is exceeding fond of you."

"And I of her."

"But I cannot seem to make myself fall in love with anyone, Nathan. I attempt it every Season in London and never get anywhere at all, and when Mama invites ladies here—well, I am not fond of there being ladies all over Bright. They set my nerves on edge. A man ought not marry someone who sets his nerves on edge, I think, and they all do. Or at least, they did."

"Did?" asked Lord Monmouth hopefully. "Do you mean to say that this time there is one who does not, Julius?"

"Yes. No. Yes and no. They all set my nerves on edge at first and now none of them do, because they are all acting so outrageously funny, you know. I thought I should smother from attempting not to laugh when Lady Angela shoo—shoo—shook her t-tail before taking the ch-chair I held for her this evening," he said, breaking into whoops. "D-did you s-see her, Nathan? First she shoo-shook her head from s-side to s-side and then she—then she—"

"I had to dash for the backstairs," interrupted Monmouth, his laughter equally as uninhibited as the duke's. "If I had been you and stuck behind that chair and sucking in my breath so as not to laugh, I should have swooned on the spot. Her—her gown did rrr-ripple so when she shoo-shook it!"

"Es-especially w-with the f-f-feathers she h-had sewed on back there! But I ought not make sport of them," added the duke, bringing his laughter back under control. "They are merely attempting to please me by imitating the nightingale, Margaret says. And I rather think she is correct."

"Correct to a tee."

"Just so. But I am not looking to *marry* a nightingale, Nathan. I do wish you would pass on that word to their chaperons. A nightingale would make a most inauspicious duchess."

\* \* \*

No sooner had Lord Monmouth taken his leave and the duke retired to his bedchamber, then the nightingale began to sing.

"Do not sing," said Amber, taking the bird upon his finger and stroking it tenderly. "Speak to me instead."

"Of what, Your Grace?"

"Of love."

"I cannot speak of love."

"You cannot? Why not? You sing of love. At least I imagine you to sing of love when I listen. Do you not know what love is?"

"Oh yes, I know," replied the nightingale. "Where love dwells, there dwells happiness despite a world of hardship. Where love dwells not, there sadness dwells despite a wealth of blessings."

"Yes, well, perhaps. But how does a person go about discovering love, eh? Can one send a servant out to market to purchase love as he might a sack of beans?"

"No, Your Grace."

"No. Just so. One cannot purchase love at all. Not even if one goes out to the market for oneself. One cannot simply find it just lying about either. And no one can tell you where to search for it. Love is apparently the most illusive thing a man can seek. In fact, I begin to think that love does not actually exist. It is a dream and nothing more. A dream devised by mischievous minions to set the whole world spinning and dogs to chasing their tails."

"Not so," protested the nightingale. "Love does exist. I have seen it in the eyes of men and women."

"Love? Are you certain 'twas love you saw? Perhaps it was merely an undigested clump of dinner caught in the woman's craw, or a tickle in the man's nose at the scent of some new parfume."

The nightingale stared up at him and cocked her little feathered head, as though she could not believe that such words were coming from between The Emperor's own lips.

"Well, what else am I to think?" grumbled Amber. "I have never seen love or felt it or tasted of it."

"You have lived it all your life," whispered the nightingale in shocked surprise.

"My mother's love do you mean? Yes, I will grant you. But that is not the love of which I speak, nightingale. The love of which I speak is the very stuff between men and women over which poets rhapsodize. Bah! It is all in the poets' heads, is it not? They think to draw us all into their own imagined worlds. And I should like to go," he added in a hoarse whisper. "I should like to go into their imagined worlds and taste of love and touch it and feel it, but I fear I never shall."

# SIX

The Duke of Haarinshire puzzled gravely over his daughter's letter. His bags packed, his team hitched, his outriders already mounted and waiting outside his front door, he had been just on the verge of leaving London for Bright, when the mail had arrived. Now he stood in the vestibule of his mansion in Grosvenor Square and squinted down at Elizabeth's atrocious scribbling. With one hand he pushed his tall beaver back from his brow, exposing a shock of guinea gold hair that matched his daughter's exactly. "What the devil?" he mumbled. "They have such a thing at Frickett and Dubbins? Well, I expect they might. But why the deuce does she require it? If the jewels are real, the thing will cost a veritable fortune."

Still, if he made her scribbling out correctly, it appeared that his daughter—who had been most skeptical of accepting Corinthia's invitation to Bright when it came—had undergone a change of heart, and now actually wished to marry the Duke of Amber. Well, he had known that she would once she had had the opportunity to spend a few days in The Emperor's own empire. Elizabeth was not some misty-eyed little milkmaid. Not Elizabeth. Her eyes were bright and wide open. She recognized power and wealth when she saw it, and she was not a stranger to what the wielding of both could do.

"An alliance between our families at last," the duke murmured. "The two most powerful and wealthy dukedoms in England united. Yes, that would be worth the price of Elizabeth's folderol, even if it should cost me thirty thousand pounds." But it cannot cost that much, he told himself as he folded the letter and tucked it away into the pocket of his puce riding jacket and strolled out into the morning sunshine.

"We make a stop in Oxford Street at Frickett and Dubbins before we make for the turnpike," Haarinshire announced to his coachman and outriders. "Then we are for Bright."

Lady Elizabeth, in a remarkably pretty riding habit of pale blue, stepped gracefully down the main staircase and strolled with chin high, blue eyes shining, and a smile upon her perfect Cupid's bow lips, into the breakfast room. "Good morning," she said to all present in a voice as clear and sweet as the early morning. "It is such a very fine day, that I have quite decided to ride out into the countryside. If, of course, Your Grace will be kind enough to provide me with a suitable mount," she added, swirling into the chair a footman held for her.

"Certainly, my lady," murmured Amber, gazing into those blue eyes with surprise as she settled beside him. "What sort of mount is it that you consider suitable?"

Lady Elizabeth glanced at her rejoicing mother. "Why, I do not know," she replied. "I do not wish to simply dawdle along as some young ladies do. But then again, I am not so reckless as to attempt a steed beyond my capabilities. I shall depend upon you, Your Grace, to select a horse neither too tame nor too wild. You will come with me to the stable, will you not, to suggest one or another of them?"

"Of course," Amber nodded. "I shall be pleased to do it."

"I do not wish to be thought forward," Elizabeth added, tasting the tea the footman poured for her. "I will have toast and jam and nothing more," she instructed him, sending him to the sideboard. "I do not wish to appear forward, Your Grace, but do you, perchance, care to ride with me? I should truly enjoy to have a companion. Riding is always exhilarating, but to be shown about the land by one who knows it intimately is always so much more interesting, do you not agree?"

Actually, The Emperor had always thought it much more interesting to ride about an unknown bit of land by himself and to discover something new and exciting around every bend without having some fellow along telling him what to expect next. But there was no accounting for people's preferences. He blinked thoughtfully at the young lady, lowered his coffee cup, and nodded. "It is a beautiful morning for a ride," he replied, "and I should think it delightful to accompany you."

The Dowager Duchess of Amber's right hand went to flutter at her heart; the Duchess of Haarinshire beamed in triumph; Lord Monmouth gazed up the table at Amber and winked encouragingly, but The Emperor noticed none of this. It will not prove any great imposition to ride out with the girl, Amber thought as he watched Lady Elizabeth take a delicate bite of her toast. All of the other young ladies are still abed and will not know. I shall not be thought to be betraying a preference for this particular one.

Mama was perfectly correct, thought Lady Elizabeth. I shall have the duke to myself for at least an hour, and merely because I chose to rise a bit early and breakfast at nine. Those other slugabeds will be so envious of me. They will be lamenting all day that they did not think to engage His Grace to ride with them at breakfast. "Where will we go?" she asked, smiling a most winning smile. "Have you a favorite place, Your Grace? If you do, I should very much like to see it."

Amber had been pondering that very thing. Everything about Bright was wonderful, but there was no one place that he preferred to ride above another. One could ride along the gardens and through the meadow and the wood—the gardens. What was it the nightingale had said to him about the gardens? Of course! That would be just the thing.

"I cannot believe that you are doing this!" exclaimed Lady Elizabeth, frowning down at Amber from the back of the fine black mare he had given her to ride.

"I merely thought it might intrigue you. You did say that if I had a favorite place—You do not need to come down if you do not wish to do so," replied the duke.

"No, wait. I have changed my mind," said Lady Elizabeth hastily, just as he turned away from her.

He smiled a bit, turned back, placed his hands about her waist, and lifted her easily to the ground. "We must be very quiet, I think," he said softly. "I have never done such a thing before, but I do think that silence must be requisite. We do not wish to frighten them away if they are somewhere about."

With a finger to his lips, Amber knelt beside the pool built from great chunks of broken Bright bricks and lined with ice blue tile. The water was so very clear and the tiles so very blue, that it looked quite as if the water itself were a piece of summer sky fallen to earth. Elizabeth did think to remark upon the marvelous color of the pool and the clarity of the water, but just as she inhaled a deep breath and began to do so, the duke lifted the tip of a lily pad floating upon the water and then of a sudden sprang forward, both his hands splashing into the pool and droplets of sun-warmed water spraying in all directions.

"Oh!" cried Lady Elizabeth, brushing at the droplets that had come down upon her riding skirt.

"Almost had him!" the duke exclaimed. "I never thought to actually find one under a lily pad. If I had truly thought to find one, I would have been ready for it."

"You are hoaxing me," grumbled Lady Elizabeth. "You saw a frog perhaps, or a tadpole. Just look at my skirt. The stain will never come out."

"Balderdash," replied the duke. "All that has touched you is one tiny drop, and I cannot even see where it fell."

He gazed at her with the most disdainful look upon his handsome face—as though seeing her for the very first time and disliking her on the instant. Well, that would never do. She had determined to marry him, had gone so far as to write her intentions to her papa and enlist his aid. She certainly could not have him looking at her like that. A smile climbed at once to her lips, coaxing the divine dimples into her cheeks.

"What a goose I am," she said lightly. "Of course my habit is not ruined. And what if it were? It would be but the tiniest sacrifice. Did you really see a faery beneath that leaf, Your Grace? I vow, I did not see a thing. Which way did it go?"

Amber stared at her a moment longer, then pointed toward the other side of the pool. "Swam straight across and leaped out on the other side, then dashed into the peonies."

"Oh no, into the peonies? We shall never find it there. Far too many leaves and petals."

"Do you think so?"

"Indeed," smiled Lady Elizabeth. "But perhaps, if we are watchful and move very slowly, we may discover more of them inside the buttercups. I do seem to recall that faeries sometimes nap in buttercups."

"In the morning?"

"Oh, indeed, for they do most of their work in the hours of darkness and do not settle down to sleep until the sun rises."

"I never knew that. Let us search the buttercups then." He held his hand out to her and she took it.

This is much more the thing, Lady Elizabeth thought as he led her carefully in among the flower beds. Even here at the very bottom of the garden, the flowers had tiny bells tied to them and the bells chimed.

As The Emperor and Elizabeth cautiously inspected one flower after another, the sun warmed them and the complacent drone of honey bees combined with the bells to produce a sense of peace. The two peered down into the buttercups and amongst the leaves of the lilies of the valley and pondered, laughing, over the petals of the daisies. After a considerable amount of laughter and hushing noises and even some crawling discreetly about, the duke cried "Ah-ha!" and pounced upon something amongst the primroses. Straightening, he held out his closed fist before her.

"What is it?" Elizabeth asked, making her eyes quite wide. "Have you caught one of them at last? I do hope so. The little rapscallions are much too elusive for me. No sooner do I glimpse a bit of wing and it is gone. Let me see it, do."

"No, I think not," teased Amber, for the very first time noticing the brightness of her eyes and the glow of her cheeks and the perfect Cupid's bow lips that smiled up at him.

"Oh, please do, Your Grace. Just one quick peek," begged Lady Elizabeth. She listened to herself say it and she knew it sounded just right—as it must if she was to keep the satisfied grin upon His Grace's face. He was convinced that she was having a wonderful time. And she intended to convince him of even more than that. She intended to convince him that she shared his glee in poking around amongst the flowers and playing childish games. I mean to have him and his fortune and Bright, she thought. And I will have all, even if I must pretend to believe in faeries. How absurd, that a grown man should believe in faeries! I have never believed in such things, not even when I was a child. But if I must tiptoe with him through the cone flowers like this and pretend to see the same tiny being that he sees scuttering off into the shadows beneath the budding gladiolas, I will. And I have, she added with an inward sigh. "Please, let me have just a peek," she implored him again with the most beguiling smile.

"What will you give me for a peek?" Amber asked, studying her thoughtfully, a boyish gleam in his eyes.

"I—I—What must I give, Your Grace?"

"Well, you look so lovely with your hat askew and your hair all tossled about and a bit of flower petal upon your chin." Amber could feel himself drawing closer to her, his head bending, his shoulders leaning gently forward, his lips moving closer and closer to those perfect Cupid's bow lips.

"AAAAchoooo! Ha-chooo!"

Amber sprang instantly away from the young lady.

"Pardon, Yer Grace," called Harry, the groom who had accompanied them and had been standing, unnoticed, holding their horses through the entire search. "Somethin' in m'nose."

"Just so," muttered Amber, realizing that Harry had just saved him from disaster—which, of course, Harry was there to do—and taking another step back from the admittedly alluring Lady Elizabeth. "A token," he said then, smiling. "You must give me a token, my lady. Something that is yours alone."

Without so much as a single thought, Elizabeth unpinned her grandmother's brooch from the lapel of her riding coat and pinned it on to his. "What was mine alone is now yours alone," she whispered. "Now let me see for what I have paid such a heavy price." And she took his fist into both of her small hands and cradled it tenderly as he extended one finger after another, unmaking the fist before her eyes and revealing a quick sparkle of sun on wings, a tiny whirring, a darting of light off into the shadow of the flowers.

\* \* \*

Well, it was a honey bee, Lady Elizabeth told herself as her maid helped her out of her riding habit and into a veritable wisp of a sprigged muslin garden dress. It must have been. Though why it did not sting him when he closed it in his fist so, I cannot imagine. I do hope, she added as she sat down at her vanity so that Emily might attend to her hair. I do hope that he does not persist in such whimsicality as I witnessed this morning. He will be a considerable handful as a husband if he does. I shall find myself forced to humor him from morn till night, and I am not good at whimsy. I have never been anything but practical for all my life. I do think that if he persists in chasing after faeries and inviting nightingales to sing after dinner, that the man will likely drive me mad.

Although, she thought with the tiniest smile, he is most handsome and definitely alluring. And he was going to kiss me. And I was going to allow him to do it, too! Oh, but Mama would have been most unhappy about that. Though it would have been a very good way to trap him into marrying me. I could have proclaimed that he had compromised me and that he must do the honorable thing. Still, Mama and Papa both would have been most embarrassed had I done such a thing as that. Besides, he will be mine without I compromise the poor fellow.

The Emperor was busily changing his clothes as well. He had got them quite mucked up—the sleeves of his jacket were still soggy from having plunged them into the pool, and the knees of his breeches were dirt- and grass-stained, and bits of pollen clung to everything. Farthingale, resisting the urge to inquire how the duke had got his clothes into such a state, helped him into dove gray breeches, a fresh shirt and neckcloth, and a silk waistcoat of brilliant royal blue. He held His Grace's jacket of midnight blue open for him and helped him to struggle into it, then assisted him to tug on a pair of Hessians which were so highly polished that both men could see their reflections in the toes. To these His Grace added a gleaming set of silver spurs.

"Are you going riding again, Your Grace?" Farthingale ventured to ask.

"No. I am promised to play billiards with Lord Monmouth and Lord Davenport and several other of my gentlemen guests until tea time. I shall not need you again, Farthingale, until it is time to dress for dinner."

"Yes, Your Grace," Farthingale acknowledged and, laying the soiled clothes across one arm, he departed, hoping that he had something belowstairs that would lift out the stains.

"There truly are faeries in the bottom of my garden!" exclaimed The Emperor excitedly, strolling into his bedchamber to find the nightingale hopping about upon her perch.

"You caught one of them! I saw you do it!"

"You did?"

"Indeed. I was perched in the elm beneath which your groom waited. You caught a faery in your bare hand. But then you let him go without so much as asking for a single wish, which is what you ought to have done. Faeries will purchase their freedom with wishes and not think one thing of it."

"Yes, well, I thought at that moment that perhaps the only wish that I had was coming true just then, though I had no suspicion that such a thing might happen when I first rode out."

"The only wish that you had? Already coming

true?" asked the little bird with a curious cock of her feathered head.

"Lady Elizabeth," explained the duke most unclearly.

"Lady Elizabeth?"

"Yes, yes, you know. No, you are a bird. I expect you do not know. But you were there, my lovely nightingale. You saw how Lady Elizabeth looked at me after I had caught that rascally faery. You saw—well—you saw her give me this brooch to wear," he grinned, pointing to the sapphire-encrusted pin which he had placed among the folds of his neckcloth.

"Your only wish was for Lady Elizabeth's brooch?"

"No. Never. What is a brooch? Mama has boxes full of them. It is what the brooch may portend, my dearest nightingale. How am I to make you understand? It was the look in her eyes and the nearness of her and—"

"The way she almost let you kiss her," finished the nightingale. "That is what you mean. Your only wish is to—"

"Discover love. The kind that we once discussed."

"The poets' kind of love," nodded the drab little bird. "Yes, I remember. The love that you think does not exist at all."

"But now I begin to think, my friend," grinned the duke, "that perhaps it does. I am not certain of it, mind you. But perhaps there is the very slightest chance that it does."

# SEVEN

That evening the nightingale sang again after dinner, and her song was more sweet, more enchanting than it had ever been. "Surely there is nothing so fine in all of England as our nightingale," proclaimed the dowager duchess to Lord Monmouth. "Only see how our guests sit spellbound by her songs."

"You have forgiven Julius then, for sending Neverby out to chase after a bird, have you, m'dear?" Lord Monmouth replied with a smile. "You no longer think him mad?"

"Well, of course not. He is quite as sane as anyone in this drawing room."

Lord Monmouth gazed about the chamber. Every young lady in the room wore feathers somewhere upon her person, and the most of them had got the precise cock of the nightingale's head down to perfection and were inclined to speak with their heads cocked in just that position whenever anyone engaged them in conversation. And from the far corner near the piano came the most ungodly warbling sound in three separate and not at all compatible keys. "Not difficult to be as sane as anyone in this chamber, Corinthia," he chuckled. "What is it that Julius wears pinned in the folds of his neckcloth?"

"Oh, my goodness," exclaimed the Duchess of

Haarinshire who was seated upon the sofa to Monmouth's left and could not help but overhear. "It is my mama's sapphire brooch! However does he come to possess my mama's sapphire brooch? I gave it to Elizabeth upon her coming out this very Season."

"Then I expect he got it from your Elizabeth," observed Monmouth. "I wonder how he managed that."

"I cannot think," replied the duchess. "It is most extraordinary."

"Perhaps it is a pledge of love," offered the dowager Duchess of Amber hopefully. "Perhaps when they rode together this very morning they came to some understanding. Oh, would not that be wonderful?"

"Wonderful indeed," nodded the duchess. "But I do think that Elizabeth might have mentioned something about such an arrangement to me, do not you, Corinthia?"

"Not if it is a secret between them."

"Never," murmured Lord Monmouth. "Julius and Lady Elizabeth are both much too proper to be keeping secrets of such magnitude from their families. It signifies something else altogether, I think. If you ladies will pardon me, I shall go and speak to the lad." And the Earl of Monmouth did just that.

"I asked for it and she gave it to me, Nathan," explained the duke as he accompanied Lord Monmouth out onto the balcony. "It was a token in payment for—"

"For what, lad?"

"Well, for showing her the faery I had captured, though the little thing flew away so very quickly that I doubt she saw much of him at all."

"A f-faery?" asked Monmouth. "Julius, a faery?"

"Just so. Caught it. Showed it to her. Set it free.

There are any of number of them living in the flowers at the bottom of the gardens."

"How do you—what made you—why would you go looking for f-faeries in the bottom of your gardens?"

"Well, the nightingale told me they were there, you see. I did not at first believe her. But then this morning, after Lady Elizabeth and I rode about a bit, I decided to see for myself if it were true and—"

"The nightingale *told* you?"

"Yes, of course. I should not have given it the least thought else."

"The nightingale speaks to you?"

"Well, pardon my impudence, Your Grace," sighed Neverby who appeared in his grace's bedchamber by demand much later that evening, "but you did think that *my* attics were to let when I said to you that the nightingale spoke."

"Yes, but I did not insist that you go immediately to bed. And I did not send for Farthingale to help you do it. No, and I did not force vile medicine down your throat and forbid you to have your window open to the night air either. Which reminds me, Neverby, you must open the window so that my nightingale may fly back in when she has a mind to do so."

"Well, Lord Monmouth has stood in place of your father for a goodly long time, and he is concerned for you," consoled Neverby, crossing the room to open the window a bit.

"Rotworms!" mumbled His Grace.

"Oh, is it not so," agreed Neverby. "Still, the world prefers us all alike, Your Grace, for if one sees differently from the rest, who knows but he may see what man is better off not seeing, eh?"

"Well, I cannot help it, Neverby, if there happen to be faeries in the bottom of my gardens. No. And I cannot be held responsible for a nightingale who speaks the King's English as properly and clearly as you and I, either. And I will not be treated like an invalid because of it. Especially not now. I want brandy, Neverby, an entire decanter filled with it. And a glass," The Emperor added, climbing from his bed and slipping into his robe. "And I am going to drink every bit of it sitting in my chair in my sitting room," he proclaimed, stalking into the adjoining chamber, "and staring into my fire. My—fire. Neverby, where the devil is my fire?"

"It is June, Your Grace," answered Neverby, about to exit the chamber in search of a full brandy decanter.

"I *know* it is June. And I have had a fire in this chamber since the month began. What happened to Tim? He is not ill?" The Emperor asked with some concern.

"No, Your Grace."

"Good. Send him up then to practice building his fire."

"Rotworms!" muttered Neverby, who had just that very evening convinced the child that he was not to start any more fires in any hearths whatsoever until the beginning of September at the very soonest. "Rotworms!"

Tim and the brandy both arrived, the fire was lit in the hearth and inside The Emperor at one and the same time, and the night faded into morning amongst a goodly number of dreams inside the Duke of Amber's head. Most of them were haunted by visions of Lady Elizabeth's smile and her Cupid's bow lips which came ever closer to his own, but never did quite kiss him. Just as the sun began to glimmer over the horizon, Amber awakened to the sound of the nightingale fluttering in through the bedchamber window. He rose, rather unsteadily, from his chair and went to see her. "Come into the sitting room," he invited in as gentlemanly a fashion as he could manage. "I am getting foxed, my dear. You shall bear me company."

"Getting foxed?" replied the bird. "You will pardon my noticing, Your Grace, but apparently you have been foxed for a prodigious number of hours and are only now getting unfoxed."

"Yes, well, I expect that is correct. I only now awoke. But the decanter is not empty. At least, I do not think it is. And I did tell Neverby that I intended to finish every last drop of it. And I do *not* lie!"

"Someone has accused you of lying, Your Grace?"

"No, no, not exactly. But Mama and Nathan do not believe me about the f-faeries. No, nor that you can speak. They think I am ill. But I am not."

"No," murmured the nightingale, fluttering onto his shoulder and pecking tenderly at his cheek. "You are not ill, Your Grace."

"No, I ain't! And I will not be treated like a child either. What must Lady Elizabeth think to see me sent off to my bed like an infant? She will not want anything to do with me now."

"Lady Elizabeth desires you whether you are treated like a child or not," the nightingale said, fluttering from His Grace's shoulder to the very top of his head as he made his way, with some overbalanced side-stepping, back into the sitting room and took up his chair before the hearth.

"Do you think she does? She was not very gracious

at all when I first took her to the bottom of the gardens, but then—then—she began to help me search and she giggled and laughed and she—well—you were there. You know. She almost let me kiss her. That must mean something, to almost let me kiss her. Do you think that Lady Elizabeth loves me, nightingale? Do you think, perhaps, that I love her?"

"I think there are certain things about you which Lady Elizabeth finds most attractive, and particular things about her which start your heart to pumping, Your Grace."

"Yes, but does that lead to love?"

"You do love, Your Grace. You are loved. You have always loved and you have always been loved and you will love forever and be loved equally as long."

"Pah! You are the one sounds chirping merry, my nightingale. Or do you speak a riddle? By whom am I loved? And do not say my mama, no, nor Nathan either."

"I cannot tell you, Your Grace. You must discover the answer for yourself," the nightingale replied and tugged one dark molasses-colored strand of hair from his head with her beak and flew off to her perch in the bedchamber.

"Ouch!" cried the duke the moment she did it. "What the devil did you do that for?" But since he did not rise from his chair and chase after her, she did not deign to answer him.


It was quite the middle of the following afternoon when the Duke of Haarinshire arrived at Bright. His coach and six came racing up the long drive across the meadow and through the gardens and up to the very front stoop of the house. Because he was in particularly good spirits, he had caused the fellow who rode beside his coachman to blow upon a fox horn the entire way from the main road and so, by the time they reached the front stoop, everyone at Bright was outside to greet them. He stepped down from his coach amid many welcomes and swept his wife into his arms and then did the same with his daughter.

"Father, have you brought it?" Lady Elizabeth whispered in his ear as she hugged him.

"Oh, yes," replied her papa. "A fine father I should be to deny anything to a daughter who intends to further my good fortune by marrying the Duke of Amber."

"Shhh, Papa. He does not know as yet."

"No? Well, but he will know soon, I think."

And then the duke set his daughter aside and, stepping forward, offered his gloved hand to The Emperor. "You have taken fine care of my darling daughter and my duchess as well, eh, Amber? I do appreciate it. Wondered what I was to do with them until I had completed my business in London. And Corinthia, how lovely you look, m'dear. And Monmouth. And Davenport."

Guessing correctly that the Duke of Haarinshire intended to prove to the group gathered before the stoop that he recognized each and every one of them, the Duke of Amber grinned and stepped aside, watching to see that his footmen managed to gather all of the portmanteaux and the trunk that Haarinshire had brought and checking to see that his grooms were running up from the stables to take the coach horses in hand and welcome coachman and guard and outriders to Bright in their own way.

He stood alone to the side, however, for a moment only, for just as he took note of Harry and Jolly and George running up the path, he felt someone take his arm and looked down to discover Lady Elizabeth looking up at him. How blue her eyes are, he thought to himself. And how they sparkle. And how perfect are those lips and red as cherries. If I kissed them, would they taste like cherries?

"Oh, Your Grace, do not gaze at me so," Lady Elizabeth said, giving his arm a gentle shake. "You look like a wolf about to devour me."

"No, I do not," laughed Amber. "Do I?"

"Most assuredly. I cannot wait until Papa's things are unpacked and he is all settled in. He has brought you the most wonderful surprise."

"He has? But why?"

"Because he is fond of you, of course."

Margaret watched them from the stoop and wondered just what Lady Elizabeth could be saying to her cousin. Whatever it was, it must be most amusing, because Julius was beaming from ear to ear.

"Really, she is the most forward thing," muttered Miss Antoinette Falsworth close behind Margaret. "If I were to step out after His Grace so and take his arm in that manner, my Aunt Beatrice would be mortified."

"Well, but Elizabeth is the daughter of a duke," Margaret said consolingly, taking Miss Falsworth's hand into her own. "She is not so intimidated by my cousin's title as are the rest of you. Come and stroll with me in the gardens for a bit, Antoinette, and we shall listen to the breezes blow and the flowers chime, and you will not be so very sad when we return, I promise you."

The two young ladies, stepping away from the bustle of the Duke of Haarinshire's arrival, wandered along the little stone paths deep into the heart of the gardens with the afternoon sunshine bearing them company. Like two sweet flowers themselves, Margaret in an afternoon dress of willow green with ribands of forest green and gold to trim it and Miss Falsworth all in pink with ivory ruffles, traipsed along together beneath parasols as delicate as hyacinths.

"You look so very unhappy," Margaret murmured. "Has Julius done something to hurt you, my dear?"

"Oh, no! Never! He is everything that is polite and kind."

"Just so," smiled Margaret, remembering her cousin's need to dash away whenever Miss Falsworth attempted to gurgle her words so as not to burst into whoops before her and make her feel embarrassed. "I know that Julius would never intentionally cause pain to anyone. But still, you are sad."

"It is because I wish to gain his attention and I cannot. I am not at all beautiful enough to appeal to such a handsome gentleman as your cousin."

"Balderdash! You are lovely."

"His Grace does not think so."

"I shall tell you a secret. His Grace does never find one young lady any more lovely than another."

"He does not?"

"No. Julius thinks you are all quite beautiful, and witty and most amusing."

"He does? Even—even me?"

"Indeed. But he is very shy at times around ladies. Why, last year Aunt Corinthia held house parties without stop straight through until October, I believe, and Julius read nearly every book in his library."

Miss Falsworth looked at Margaret in the most curious fashion. "He read nearly—?"

"Because he was so very nervous about meeting and entertaining all the guests—well, not the gentlemen, but the young ladies—that he hid in the library for days on end."

Miss Falsworth giggled.

"Just so," nodded Margaret and grinned. "It is because Elizabeth is so forward with him that he notices her a bit more than the rest of you. If you were to take his arm, he would smile down just as kindly at you. But that is neither here nor there, because you do not truly wish to marry my cousin, do you?"

"I—I have not thought—that is to say—"

"Come now, Antoinette. We have known each other for almost three whole weeks, and I know you do not truly wish to marry Julius. He frightens you."

"But Aunt Beatrice says that I *ought* to wish to marry him."

"Humbug!"

"Humbug?"

"Yes, indeed, humbug! No one ought to marry someone who frightens them. What a horrible life one must live then."

"But he is a duke and wealthy and handsome."

"Jeremy, Lord Trevane, is not a duke, but he is handsome and is generally considered to have very deep pockets."

"Lord Trevane? The gentleman who sat beside me at dinner last evening?"

"Precisely. He is Miss Scott's brother, and he has been following you about all over Bright hoping that you might take some particular notice of him. He begged me to rearrange the seating last evening so that he might dine on your right. I ought not be so bold as to tell you this, Antoinette, but you did look so sad and I promised to make you happy and—the truth is, my dearest, that Lord Trevane has conceived a considerable passion for you, and has spent at least four days cursing under his breath because you spend so much time attempting to please Julius that you do not notice him at all. I fear it will come to swordplay if you do not redirect your attentions. I truly do. And poor Julius will not even know why he is facing Lord Trevane across a green."

"Can this be true?" asked Miss Falsworth, her dark eyes aglow with wonder. "Lord Trevane has developed a passion for me?"

"Entirely true," laughed Margaret, leading Miss Falsworth back toward the house. "Every summer some lady and some gentleman fall in love at Bright during one of the house parties. Last year there were three couples married by September."

"Oh!" Miss Falsworth exclaimed gleefully. "It is magic!"

"In a way," nodded Margaret. But it is a very fickle magic, she added in silence. It never seems to work for Julius.

# EIGHT

Lady Elizabeth, while her papa smiled and her mama beamed, stepped up to the Duke of Amber shortly after the gentlemen joined the ladies in the withdraw room that evening. In her hand she held a package wrapped in silver paper. "For you, Your Grace," she said, her eyes flashing up at him through slightly lowered lashes. "It is the surprise I mentioned that Papa brought with him. Papa and Mama and I hope that it pleases you."

The Emperor's ears reddened the slightest bit. "Truly, there was no need—"

"We wish you to have it," the Duke of Haarinshire declared. "Do not be shy, lad. Open the thing up. It is a trifle merely."

Everyone's attention centered upon the Duke of Amber and the package. Young ladies twittered. Gentlemen buzzed. It was most unusual for one duke to present another with a present so publicly, and even more unusual that Haarinshire should select his daughter to give the thing into Amber's hands.

Neverby, unobtrusively lighting the candelabra upon the pianoforte at the far end of the room, paused to watch as his master fiddled with the silver paper. The little nightingale beside him bobbed up and down upon her perch, for all the world as if she were curious to see what the package held herself.

The entire room became silent as the silver wrapping fell to the floor and The Emperor lifted the lid from an extremely beautiful and painted box. He peered down into it and gasped. He set the box down upon a cherrywood cricket table and lifted the present carefully from it. The thing sparkled and pulsed in the candlelight. Like Bright itself on a sunny day, it glowed with brilliant reds and blues and greens and crystal whites.

"It is a nightingale," Lady Elizabeth told him needlessly. "Is it not the most beautiful thing you have ever seen?"

The Duke of Amber nodded, unable to think of a word to say in the face of the jewel-encrusted bird. "I—I—thank you very much," he murmured at last, gazing into Lady Elizabeth's thoroughly triumphant face and then turning to include the Duke and Duchess of Haarinshire in his expression of gratitude. "But I cannot possibly accept such a—"

"Of course you can," interrupted Lady Elizabeth.

"But—but—" What Amber thought to say was that the bird, fashioned from gold and studded with rubies, emeralds, sapphires, and diamonds must have cost Haarinshire a King's ransom, and that Haarinshire must be out of his mind to bestow such a gift upon him. Of course, he could not say that.

"It is not merely a trinket to set upon your mantel," Lady Elizabeth explained gaily, reaching down into the box and lifting from it a golden key. "It is mechanical, Your Grace. It sings! You need merely wind it up, and it will warble the most beautiful songs for you. Try it," she urged, placing the key into the duke's hand.

"Wind it up, Your Grace," called several of the gentlemen.

"Yes, wind it up, do," nodded the Duke of Haarinshire. "I have not heard it as yet."

The Duke of Amber's gaze wandered far across the room to the little nightingale bobbing upon her perch, awaiting her time to sing after dinner. His eyes caught a sudden frown flicker across Neverby's distant countenance. Then he looked upon the smiling Lady Elizabeth and her fondly beaming parents. With some hesitancy, he placed the golden key into a slot at the base of the golden perch upon which the bejeweled nightingale sat, and began to wind the springs inside. When the key refused to turn farther, he stared at the bird, waiting.

"There must be a lever you throw," offered Haarinshire. "Yes, here it is," he nodded, placing a finger upon a small mechanism beneath the nightingale's breast. The Duke of Haarinshire flipped the thing, and the mechanical bird began to bob its head and its tail moved rhythmically up and down and its golden beak opened and closed and it began to sing.

"Amazing," breathed Lord Monmouth, rising from his place beside the dowager duchess and striding to Amber's side.

"Unbelievable," murmured Lady Angelica Davenport's mama and, tugging her daughter with her, hurried to get a closer view of the marvelous toy.

"I have never seen anything at all like it," Margaret acknowledged, moving closer to her cousin. "Julius, it sings waltzes!"

"Y-yes," stuttered The Emperor, staring at the nightingale in his hand as it warbled away, its sapphire eyes unblinking but aglow. "It s–sings w-waltzes."

"How perfectly lovely," declared his mama then, from the sofa. "Bring it here, Julius, that I may see it more clearly. Ta-de-de-da-dum," she added, marking the time with one finger. "I recognize that melody, Julius. It was played over and over at the balls this Season. All the young people wished to dance to it."

The Duke of Amber carried the mechanical nightingale to his mama and set it upon the low table before the sofa. Absolutely every one of the guests gathered around to watch the jewels sparkle and the head bob and the tail move up and down and the little beak open and close as it sang. And when it had finished the first of the waltzes, it whirred for an instant, and then began to sing a second one.

Lady Elizabeth once again took The Emperor's arm and laughing, praised the trifle to the skies. Miss Scott and Miss Falsworth and all the young ladies and all their mamas and papas and aunts and grandmothers and even Miss Scott's brother had nothing but superlatives to say about it.

"And it is so much better than the real nightingale," proclaimed Lady Elizabeth at the last, "because it sings songs that everyone knows. Why one can sing right along with it, and the rhythms are so perfectly timed that one may dance to them. The music is not at all so oddly phrased as is the music of the real nightingale. And the jewels are so much more beautiful than the real nightingale's drab old feathers."

In the far corner of the drawing room near the pianoforte, the real nightingale fluttered her wings and ruffled her feathers and hopped from foot to foot. No one took the least note of her but Neverby, who shook his head from side to side and muttered "Rotworms!" very softly.

The Emperor's new nightingale instantly became the rage of the house party. Everyone wished to wind it up. Everyone wished to move the lever. Everyone wished to hold it and inspect it and gaze upon the jewels. Over and over again it sang the very same three songs as it traveled from hand to hand. It sang those three songs thirty-two times in a row, until everyone had them by heart. And that was considered a decided plus, for if one knew the songs by heart, then one might sing forth loudly right along with the nightingale, and everyone did. The servants, one by one, tiptoed to the threshold of the drawing room and listened to the mechanical bird and dubbed it "the most extraordinary thing."

But the Duke of Amber was not at all certain that he liked the mechanical nightingale. Certainly it was a great deal prettier than the drab little bird who had come to him from the wood. It shone in the candlelight like the crown jewels. And anyone could see how expensive it was, and it was so unique as to fit in quite perfectly with all the other unique things about Bright. But when it sang, The Emperor heard nothing he had not heard before—nothing that made his heart swell or brought tears to his eyes. "Enough," he said as Lady Elizabeth was about to turn the golden key for the thirty-third time. "It is time, I think, to hear the real nightingale sing."

"I have the most marvelous idea," declared Lady Elizabeth. "I shall wind up this nightingale and the two shall sing together. That will be something to hear."

Amber nodded and Lady Elizabeth wound up the bejeweled bird as Neverby, at a sign from the duke, brought the little nightingale and her perch into the very center of the room. No sooner did the mechanical nightingale begin to whirr into song, than the real nightingale opened her beak and began to warble. The sound of the two together was most distressing and absolutely everyone in the drawing room put their hands over their ears.

"It is because the mechanical bird has a set tone and rhythm and does not vary from it, while the real nightingale sings whatever she feels," the Duke of Haarinshire explained, once the singing had ceased.

"That is precisely why a mechanical bird is so much better," declared Lady Elizabeth. "One knows exactly what one will hear."

"Indeed," nodded the eldest of the Templeton-Smith sisters. "And one may take the thing apart and discover exactly how it is put together and what makes the songs come out. You cannot do that with a real bird. There is no discovering at all what makes a real nightingale sing."

"And the mechanical nightingale's plumage is ever so much more attractive," added Lady Angela Davenport, blowing one of the feathers from her headpiece away from her cheek. She could not help but think how much nicer it would be to bedeck herself in jewels in order to copy the mechanical nightingale, rather than to bedeck herself in feathers from morn till night.

"The mechanical nightingale is most definitely an

improvement upon the real thing," the dowager duchess declared.

"Perhaps," drawled The Emperor slowly, studying the approving faces of those around him, "but I should still like to hear my nightingale sing again—all by herself." He turned away from the jeweled prize and looked to the perch in the very center of the drawing room and found it empty. "Neverby," he asked, "where has my nightingale gone?"

"Flew out the window, Your Grace, while everyone was discussing that one," Neverby replied softly. "I could not catch her, Your Grace. She was perched right here, but then I looked to see the candlelight sparkling upon the golden nightingale and when I turned back, she was out the window and disappearing into the night."

"What an ungrateful bird!" exclaimed Lady Elizabeth. "How she treat His Grace so! To fly away from him and just when he wished to have her sing, too! Never mind, Your Grace," she added, taking his hand and drawing him down to sit upon the arm of her chair. "This nightingale will never be so dastardly as that one. This nightingale will remain with you forever."

"Yes, it certainly will," agreed the gentlemen gathered about it. "It cannot possibly fly away. It must remain wherever one puts it."

"And one may have a song from it at any time," smiled Lady Elizabeth.

"And it will never put one to the expense of room and board," grinned Lord Monmouth. "All this bird requires is a place to sit and a maid to dust it off from time to time."

"And it is the verimost beautiful thing in all the

world," the ladies chimed in. "A pleasure to look upon and delightful to hear. What can be better than that?"

"Nothing can be better than that," Lady Elizabeth assured The Emperor, and she smiled up at him with the most beguiling smile she could manage and gave his hand a most encouraging pat.

Julius Caesar Crofton could not sleep. He wished for sleep. He longed for sleep. But it would not come. It occurred to him that perhaps he missed speaking with the nightingale, and sitting up in his bed and yawning, he reached out and turned the golden key of the mechanical nightingale which sat on a red velvet pillow upon the nightstand beside his bed. He flipped its lever and true as ever, the bird began to bob its head and move its tail up and down and then it opened its little beak and warbled a perfect waltz. The Emperor lay back down and hummed along with it. His guests had been correct about one thing. He could never have hummed along with the song of the real nightingale. And if the mechanical bird did not make his heart soar with the pure sweetness and pathos of its music, if it did not stir him so that tears mounted unbidden to his eyes, it did do something else. It made him feel contented and happy.

He wound the mechanism and he hummed. He wound the mechanism and he hummed. Over and over again he wound and hummed and wound and hummed, but he did not sleep. His thoughts, instead, wandered over the past few weeks. Visions of Lady Elizabeth with her wide blue eyes and her guinea gold hair and her Cupid's bow lips waltzed in his brain. He saw her speaking and walking and riding, smiling and giggling and laughing. Truly, she was as beautiful as the nightingale she had placed into his hands, and no doubt she would make him equally as contented and happy. She would stay with him if he asked it of her. Unlike Fiona so long ago and the nightingale from the wood this very night, neither the mechanical nightingale nor Lady Elizabeth would ever just fly away and leave him behind to wonder where they had gone.

"And perhaps that is all that one can expect of love," he murmured, "to possess someone who is beautiful, whom others admire, someone who makes you content and happy. Perhaps that and knowing that the one you possess cannot fly off into the night is all there is to love, and the rest is merely poetry."

The very next morning, His Grace, Julius Caesar Crofton rose with the dawn and dressed in his very best morning coat. He broke his fast alone before his mama or any of the guests had reached the table, and he went to wander among the flowers of his gardens. They chimed at him from time to time as he strolled along the cobbled paths. Once or twice he stopped to listen. But for the most part he continued walking, his feet carrying him all the way to the bottom of the gardens. Here he paused and peered down into the pool. He peeked under the lily pads. He bent and inspected the insides of blossoms and the undersides of leaves.

"Just as I suspected," he whispered to himself. "All nonsense. There are no faeries here. Perhaps Mama and Nathan were correct. Perhaps I was ill for a time."

But I am well now, he thought, shoving his hands into the pockets of his breeches, and I am quite posi-

tive that there are no such things as faeries—especially
not in the bottom of *my* gardens—no, and though
nightingales do exist, they are quite common birds
and sing quite common songs that are not even
waltzes. "And they do not speak," he added with a
sigh. "How did I grow so mad as to think a nightingale
spoke to me?"

The Emperor, seeing that the sun had, by this time,
risen high into the summer sky, strolled back up
through the gardens to Bright and let himself inside
through the French doors leading into the library. He
crossed to the bellpull and gave it a tug. When Neverby
arrived, he sent the butler scurrying off to discover if
the Duke of Haarinshire was up and about.

"If he is, Neverby, say that I require to speak with
him, if you please, whenever he has a free moment. I
shall await him here. And bring me some tea, Neverby,
eh? A pot of black tea."

Lady Elizabeth was breakfasting alone with her papa
when the duke's message came. "Oh, Papa," she
gasped, "His Grace wishes to speak with you alone! It
can only mean one thing!"

The Duke of Haarinshire smiled hopefully. "Do you
think so, Elizabeth? Perhaps he simply wishes my ad-
vice about a horse or a purchase of some new equipment? Or perhaps he wishes to discuss the present
unrest over the Corn Laws?"

"Oh, no, Papa, I am certain not. Why he could discuss such things with you in the presence of all the
other gentlemen. He is going to ask your permission
to address me, Papa! I know he is!"

"And what am I to say, my Elizabeth, now that I have

sunk a veritable fortune into this venture by the purchase of that shimmering nightingale? Do you still intend to have the man? I hope you do, or else I have wasted near one thousand pounds on a mere trifle of a music box."

"Yes, Papa," nodded Lady Elizabeth, her eyes shining. "I do intend to have him. He is a bit whimsical and that I hope will change, but he is quite handsome, Papa."

"Ah, yes, and will you marry him because he is so handsome?"

"Well, of course it is important to *be* handsome. How would it look should I marry some ugly, bent, and limping gentleman? I could not bear to face any of my friends did I do such a thing as that, Papa. But he is very wealthy as well. Wealthier, I think, than ever anyone dreamed to be. All you need do is to look around you, Papa, to see what it is like to have pockets that extend into infinity."

The Duke of Haarinshire nodded. This was the daughter he had raised. She knew the value of a penny, Elizabeth did, and knew well how to spend it, too.

"And he is very powerful as well, I think."

"Very powerful," the duke agreed. "Amber wields the power not only of his wealth, but of a lineage of warrior-rulers conceived among the ancients. And all of England recognizes that, my dear. There is no one will go against him once his mind is set. And a wife may set a husband's mind upon certain things, you know. Wives may wield their husbands' power by a word here or a frown there or a sigh or a smile."

"Yes, Papa, I know. I shall be the Duchess of Amber, a leader of Society and courted by absolutely everyone."

"Just so," smiled her papa, setting aside his napkin and rising from his chair. "I expect I shall go and converse with The Emperor then, eh? And see what it is that is on his mind?"

# NINE

No sooner had The Emperor spoken to the Duke of Haarinshire than he spoke as well to Lady Elizabeth. And she, as her mama and papa had known she would, accepted his proposal of marriage. The announcement of their engagement was made to the entire house party that evening when they had gathered for dinner, and the bejeweled nightingale was brought into the dining room upon a red velvet cushion and wound up and made to sing through the entire meal. Then it sang in the drawing room after dinner. And when the house party guests departed for their own homes the following day, the nightingale sat conspicuously upon the newel post in the vestibule and the golden bird with its rubies and sapphires, emeralds and diamonds, sang each guest on his or her way with a perfectly measured waltz.

"I cannot believe it, Julius," smiled the dowager duchess when everyone was gone and she came to sit beside her son in the coziness of a tiny room off the main parlor. "You are to be married! We must send notices to all of the London newspapers, and the banns must be read. Oh, my dearest, I am so very happy for you, that you have found love at last."

"Yes, Mama," nodded the duke, winding the nightingale tightly and setting it down upon the table beside him to sing.

"And I am so very happy that Lady Elizabeth wishes to have the wedding here at Bright. Bright was built for weddings. Your papa and I were married here, you know. And your grandmama and grandpapa. And now, you shall do the same. Oh, it is so wonderful!"

The duke nodded again. He wondered at it, that Lady Elizabeth should prefer to be married from Bright rather than from her own home, but she had been very clear about the thing. He had even suggested to her that he would not at all mind traveling into Hertfordshire to her papa's main residence to repeat the vows, but she would not hear of it.

"Oh, never, Julius darling," she had said, both her hands clinging to his arm. "The gardens will be so beautiful in August, and Bright will shimmer so in the sunlight. It will be quite like a faery tale. I should not wish to be married anywhere else."

She did not add, thought His Grace, that all the expense of housing and entertaining the wedding guests and decorating for the thing and holding the wedding breakfast will fall upon my shoulders and not her papa's. But that was a most unkind thing to think, and so he shook his head and sent the thought slipping out his ear. Elizabeth was to be his wife and he would not allow himself to think anything at all unkind about her or about her family—though he had not failed to notice the slight but greedy flaring of the Duke of Haarinshire's nostrils and the triumphant gleam in his eyes when a cask of amontillado had been tapped and distributed among the guests to toast the happy couple, or the unchecked smile of victory upon the Duchess of Haarinshire's face when he had clasped his grandmama's necklace of diamonds and sapphires about Elizabeth's neck as a betrothal gift.

They are merely contemplating the benefits of the match and looking forward to the alliance of our families and that is all, Amber told himself, rising from his chair and beginning to pace the room, turning his mama's ecstatic countenance into a questioning gaze.

"Julius, you do *wish* to marry the girl?"

"Yes, Mama. It is well past time, I think, to settle down and beget you a grandchild."

"Just so."

"And I expect you will be pleased to be free of me at last. No, no, do not protest, Mama. I know that you have remained at Bright simply to run my household and that you would rather join Lord Monmouth at Monmouth Hall and run his household instead."

"Oh, Julius, that is not—"

"I know you wish to marry Nathan, Mama, and have wished to do so since Lady Monmouth died of the influenza. I think that I have kept the two of you apart long enough. I expect you will be married before Elizabeth and I return from our wedding trip, will you not?"

The dowager duchess colored up prettily.

"Just so," nodded Amber. "And that is as it should be. You ought not have continued on alone for so long as you have done. But if you do not mind, Mama, I would prefer not to discuss weddings for awhile yet. I should like to forget all about weddings until it is absolutely necessary that I think of them." And the duke crossed back to the table upon which the mechanical nightingale sat, wound it up again, and set it to singing. Then, stuffing his hands into his breeches' pockets, he strolled with his head lowered from the room.

\* \* \*

The mechanical nightingale sang morning, noon, and night. It sang for The Emperor at breakfast and warbled the day away with him while he sat over his books in the library. Sometimes Amber would even hand the bird into Neverby's care and send him with it down to the kitchen, or to the servants' little dining room. Once or twice the duke went so far as to send it out to sing for the stablehands and the horses and then urged Neverby to carry it to the head gardener's cottage and make it sing for him.

"And did they all enjoy it?" he would ask whenever Neverby returned from one of his musical excursions.

"Indeed, Your Grace," Neverby would reply. "Everyone thinks it the most splendid thing."

"You did not happen to—to hear—the real nightingale while you were out, did you, Neverby?" the duke would query then.

"No, Your Grace," Neverby would reply with a shake of his head. "I have not heard the real nightingale since she flew from the drawing room that evening."

The very first week of August brought hot, heavy weather and a plethora of storm clouds. Each day about noon the sky would darken and thunder would rumble across the tiny Empire of Amber, and then lightning would spark the air and the clouds would open and the rain pour down. It was during one of these afternoon thundershowers, while Amber was sitting alone in his library attempting to drive the nervousness that he felt concerning his approaching nuptials from his mind, that he reached over to the nightingale which sat on its red velvet cushion upon the cricket table beside him and wound it up. *Whirrr,* it went. *Whirr bzst zip!* And then it went *Bong!!!* and the nightingale's beak opened and its head nodded just the slightest bit to the left and its tail tilted just the merest bit to the right and there it sat, not moving, not singing, not doing anything at all.

"Neverby!" The Emperor shouted, not even bothering to go to the bellpull, but hurrying to the door instead and calling out into the corridor. "Neverby! Come to me at once!"

Well, not only did Neverby come rushing as fast as his feet would carry him, but the duke's mama came running to see what had happened and every footman within hearing of the duke's bellow, and every little maid who thought she might be of some assistance, and the library filled with people who all stared in horror at the silent nightingale with its beak open and its head nodded just the slightest bit to the left and its tail tilted just the merest bit to the right. A discussion ensued upon the spot as to what could be done and at the conclusion of it, James, the first footman, was dispatched to Minor-Glistening-on-the-Stream in His Grace's coach and returned just as the thunderstorm ended with the jeweler and the clockmaker both.

"Such a marvelous trinket!" exclaimed the jeweler, examining the rubies and sapphires, the diamonds and emeralds set into the gold. "The work of a master!"

"Elegant," agreed the clockmaker.

They passed the bird between them, from one to the other and back again. The jeweler stared at it through his eyepiece. The clockmaker held it upside down and shook it beside his ear.

"It will need to be taken all to pieces," they agreed at last, and they did just that, scattering the springs and gears and gadgets that were the nightingale's little insides all over The Emperor's library table, as the duke and his mama and Neverby and James looked on.

"Hmmmmm," the jeweler said.

"Ahhhh," murmured the clockmaker.

"Very worn," the jeweler mumbled, with a shake of his head.

"Almost beyond repair," agreed the clockmaker, stroking his chin thoughtfully.

"But you can repair it?" asked the dowager duchess with a sad trembling of her lips. "You can make it sing again? It must sing at my son's wedding. My daughter-in-law-to-be will expect to see it there and to hear it, too."

"It does not matter, Mama," sighed Amber. "Elizabeth will marry me, I think, whether the nightingale appears or whether it does not."

"Most certainly she will. But she will be most disappointed to find the nightingale is broken."

The jeweler lifted a gear to his eyepiece and *hmmmmmed*.

The clockmaker stroked a spring and *ahhhhhhed*.

The dowager duchess clasped her hands together before her and stood staring fearfully down at the mechanical nightingale's insides. James, the first footman, did the same. The Duke of Amber began to pace aimlessly about the library, gazing from time to time in the direction of the library table where the surgery upon the bejeweled bird progressed, and Neverby stuffed his hands into his pockets in a most unbutler-like fashion and mumbled "Rotworms!"

The entire operation lasted a good three hours, and when at last the nightingale sat once more upon its red velvet cushion, it looked quite as marvelous as it always had.

"But you must wind it up only sparingly," warned the jeweler with a thoughtful scowl.

"The gears are worn and the springs as well, and if it is made to sing too often, it will break again, and there will be no fixing it then," added the clockmaker.

The Emperor nodded, paid them each a handsome sum, and sent them on their way.

Neverby removed the nightingale to the duke's chambers and set it safely upon the table beside his bed. He stared down at the bird which glittered enticingly in the glow of the lamplight, and muttered "Rotworms!"

Margaret arrived on the following Friday to assist her Aunt Corinthia in preparing the household for the arrival of Lady Elizabeth and her mama and papa and the plethora of wedding guests who were to begin descending upon Bright on Tuesday. When she learned the fate of the mechanical nightingale, she gave her cousin's shoulder a consoling pat and assured him that even if it could no longer be depended upon to sing at his every whim, still it was a beautiful trinket and worth having merely to gaze upon.

Lady Elizabeth, when she arrived, was not quite so understanding. "Do you mean to say that you have broken it?" she asked, staring up at Amber with her hands fisted upon her hips. "Well, of all things. You are worse than an infant. There is not another one to be had in all of England, Julius!"

"It still sings, Elizabeth," the duke replied, considering the beautiful face before him gravely. "We must simply not expect it to sing constantly. It has springs and gears and gadgets, you know, and they do tend to wear out."

This, Lady Elizabeth conceded, was necessarily the case, and her hands unfisted and left her hips to go about Amber's neck as she gave him a gentle kiss upon the cheek. "I am so sorry, Julius my dear, she whispered, remembering who he was and who she was and how much she desired to become mistress of Bright. "I ought not to have spoken to you so. It will sing once, after all of our guests have arrived, and once at our wedding. That will not overtax its mechanisms, will it? No. Of course it will not. Come, dearest, and let us stroll through the gardens while the sun shines so warmly. We shall select the perfect spot in which to take our vows."

"We are getting married in the gardens?"

"Well, of course."

"I thought—well, it does not matter, I expect, unless it should rain."

"If it rains, we shall do the deed in the long drawing room before the windows. I have already checked, and it will be quite large enough to accommodate every one of our guests," Lady Elizabeth smiled, seizing his arm and steering him out through the French doors, across a tiny patio and down two steps into the gardens. "It is not to be a large wedding after all. We do not require a place the size of St. Paul's. I am so very glad it is to be a small ceremony, are not you? I would find all the pomp and circumstance of a large one most dreadful."

"You would?" This astounded the duke somewhat, for he had formed the opinion that his bride-to-be quite delighted in pomp and circumstance.

"Oh, yes. And besides, if we did wish to marry in St. Paul's with absolutely everyone of importance in attendance, we should need to put the ceremony off until next spring when all of the *ton* are gathered again in London."

The Duke of Amber nodded. "You wish to be married sooner than later," he murmured.

"Well, of course. That is precisely what we decided upon."

Amber could not quite remember deciding upon anything except to ask Elizabeth to marry him. The rest had seemed to occur 'round about him without the least inquiry into his preferences. Still, he did not much care. To be married in August in the gardens of Bright was just as fine as to be married in London in the middle of the Season. "Just so you are happy, my dear," he said, gazing down at her prettily flushed cheek as she strolled beside him. "That is all that matters, your happiness."

Lady Elizabeth nodded. Truly, she thought, he is not merely wealthy and handsome and a duke, but he is considerate of my wishes as well. He will be the most excellent of husbands. And once we have said our vows, I shall explain to him about Robert. I am certain he will not make the least fuss about Robert. Surely not. I must only handle him in the right way, and he will not have the least objection to Robert's hanging about from time to time.

And as if her merely thinking of that gentleman had made him visible, Robert, Lord Patton, appeared before them as they negotiated a turn in the path.

"Robert!" Lady Elizabeth cried. "How good to see you! When did you arrive?"

"Just a bit ago," responded the tall, sturdy gentleman, walking forward to meet them. "You are Amber, I expect," he said, thrusting his hand toward the duke. "May I congratulate you upon your coming marriage to my cousin. Elizabeth is a prize."

"Just so," Amber agreed, taking the proffered hand. "You are Elizabeth's cousin?"

"Well, third or fourth or second once-removed. We have never actually cared to investigate. It is through our mothers we are related. We have known each other from childhood."

Lady Elizabeth, her face aglow, tucked her free hand through Robert's arm and urged both gentlemen to accompany her deeper into the gardens. I shall encourage Julius to like Robert excessively, she thought, and then he will not mind to have Robert about at all, and he will never become suspicious. "Robert is most fond of flowers," she said, smiling innocently up at the duke. "He has been longing to see Bright's gardens ever since I first spoke of them. Have you not, Robert?"

"Indeed. And a grand sight they are, too, Duke. Are the horses in your stables equally as grand?"

"Everything at Bright is grand," Lady Elizabeth answered before Amber's lips could even part. "You have never seen such an extraordinary place with so many wonderful things in all of your life, Robert, I promise you. Even if you visit with us for an entire nine months out of the year, you will not have time to see everything that is remarkable about Bright."

Visit us nine months out of the year? thought Amber, studying the blond, blue-eyed gentleman who marched along at Elizabeth's right. Well, but it is merely a manner of speaking. She does not intend to invite the man to live with us. I must grow accustomed,

I think, to the extravagances in Elizabeth's way of saying things. Still, there is something odd about the gentleman marching upon Elizabeth's right. The way he smiles so ingratiatingly for one thing.

Something about that smile and the manner in which Elizabeth clung to the gentleman's arm made Amber most uneasy.

# TEN

After two days and nights of toasts and jokes, of greeting friends and friends-to-be, of praises and congratulations, shortly after a spontaneous bit of dancing had sprung up in the long drawing room following dinner, with Margaret at the pianoforte and Julius's Cousin Leonard tooting upon the French horn, the Duke of Amber wandered away from the party and into the quiet of his study where the French doors leading to the gardens stood open to the night, and the music could be heard only softly as a growing breeze fanned the flowers outside and made them chime right along with Margaret's and Leonard's playing. There were no candles lit here. Only moonlight flickered feebly as that cool silver orb peeked out from behind storm clouds now and again. It was almost impossible to see anything at all.

The Emperor fished about in his pockets for his flints, intending to light a lamp or two and then close the door to the corridor and the doors to the balcony and sit alone for a while. He needed time to ponder. He had never been so close to marriage before. Nor had he ever been, since he had gained his manhood, so very close to love. He thought that he had a good chance of achieving love—at least, something close to it—because Elizabeth had been acting so very differently toward him now that they were betrothed. She held his hand and clung to his arm and kissed his cheek every now and then, and whispered to him how dear he was to her and how much she looked forward to being his wife.

Well, and he was looking forward to being her husband, too. At first he had not been nearly so thrilled with their engagement, but now it seemed that his marriage to Elizabeth would be the very best thing that could ever happen to him, and he meant to discover some means to make her feel exactly the same way. "She truly does love me," he whispered, locating his flints and tugging them out of his pocket. "She truly does love. There is such a thing as love after all." And his heart leaped with joy in his breast and his happiness caught in his throat, and he thought what a miracle it was that the one thing he had thought never to be allowed to have should come to him, and he had not even recognized it until now.

And then, just as he was about to strike his flints, he heard the whispering. At first he was not at all certain that it was whispering. Perhaps, he thought, ceasing all movement to listen intently, perhaps it is but the wind. There is a storm on the horizon. He walked quietly toward the doors to the balcony, straining his ears, and caught the sound of a hushed giggle and more whispering. And then, as he reached the entrance to the balcony, there was no sound at all, but the moon came out fully from behind one of the clouds and the balcony swam in moonlight and in the cold silver glow of it, Amber saw a woman held tightly in a gentleman's arms. The gentleman's head was lowered to hers, kissing her, and doing a damnably good job of it, too.

He thought to turn away at once, but he could not. His eyes fixed upon the young woman's golden ringlets and the cool silk of her gown and the particularly wide bow tied at the back in a most becoming French fashion. "Elizabeth?" Her name escaped him, though he had not meant it to do so.

In the wiggle of a cat's whisker, the couple separated and Elizabeth turned to stare at him, her lips slightly parted, the sparkle of her eyes trembling in the moonlight. Lord Patton took a step backward and came up flush against the balcony rail.

"Julius, my darling," Lady Elizabeth managed breathlessly, straightening her shoulders and going to him, taking his hands into her own. "It is not at all what you think, Julius."

"No," murmured The Emperor, freeing his hands from hers.

"Robert and I—Robert and I—"

"Sorry, old man," Patton mumbled awkwardly. "Elizabeth assured me it was to be a marriage of convenience, you know, and that we might keep on as we—"

"Robert, do keep still!" hissed Elizabeth.

The Emperor merely shuddered a bit as his heart ripped wide open. "I do beg your pardon for the intrusion," he said quietly, as all of his newborn dreams of love died amidst the thunder in his ears. He made a stiff, awkward bow, walked past them both, and stepped down into the gardens. Above his head the thunder roared louder, closer, and lightning careened across the sky. The full moon faded beneath another storm cloud. On the balcony, Elizabeth, her hand to her mouth, her lips trembling, watched his back and gave the tiniest, most plaintive squeak. But he took

note of none of it. He only strolled down the first cobbled path that met his feet, looking neither to left nor
right.

He had been beyond foolish to believe in love. If it
did in fact exist, it did not exist for him. And what did
it matter if his bride-to-be had been kissing Patton
upon the balcony? Amber attempted to tell himself
that it did not matter. Not at all. But the ache in his
heart and the tears stinging his eyes proclaimed otherwise. As the rain began to fall in earnest, The Emperor
turned right and wandered toward the very bottom
of his gardens.

They did not find the Duke of Amber until after
dawn the next morning. In the darkness and the wind
and the rain, he had missed his step and fallen, hitting
his head on the edge of the little pool. Unconscious,
wet through and shivering from the damp, he never
waked, not even when they carried him back to the
house and put him warmly to bed in his own chambers. The physician was called and the surgeon.

"Hmmmm," said the physician, and wrapped a ban-
dage around the duke's bleeding brow.

"Ahhhhhhh," nodded the surgeon, and ordered
the fire to be lit in the duke's bedchamber.

But they did nothing more and left him much as
they had found him, for they overheard Lady Elizabeth sobbingly confess to her mama of her *affaire* with
Robert, who could never be her husband for he had
not a penny to his name. And they heard how The
Emperor had come to discover it. And they decided
that their learned professions would be of not the least
use now.

"His heart has shattered, I suspect," whispered the physician. "It was a good heart, but delicate at best."

"He will die, I think," agreed the surgeon. "What split asunder upon that balcony cannot be repaired by one such as I. His Grace must save himself, Dr. Quigley, for God knows that you and I cannot save him."

For two days following there were murmurs and whispers and nothing more among the wedding guests. The sounds of joy had dissipated, and the sounds of mourning not yet begun. Tears stood endlessly in Margaret's eyes, and Lord Monmouth kept a supportive arm about the dowager duchess from morning until night. The servants walked with heads lowered, their footsteps silent as they traversed the corridor outside their master's chambers. And by the night of the third day, everyone expected the Duke of Amber to breathe his last. That was why, before Neverby left his side that evening, he thought it would be all right to open His Grace's window. Just a bit. Just enough to let a breath of fresh air into the hot, stuffy room, which must be unbearable even for one so ill as His Grace.

In the great four-poster bed which had once belonged to his father, Amber lay motionless as the night began to fade into dawn. It felt to him as though a great slab of granite covered him over, and any attempt at movement would be futile. Still, he did manage to blink his eyes open at last. What he saw made him wish he had kept them shut tight.

Upon his chest sat the most hideous vision. All dressed in black, it was, with a black hood hiding the worst of its visage. Still, from deep inside that hood, Amber could make out sightless eyes that burned like hellfire. And all around that devilish vision, hiding in the folds of its cloak and the wrinkles of Amber's counterpane and the creases of the draperies about Amber's bed, the most outrageous faces peeked and peered at the duke. Some had sad, pleading eyes, and others vicious smiles and slobbering lips.

"You are Death," whispered The Emperor hoarsely to the figure who sat upon his chest.

"Just so," responded Death in a voice like logs snapping on the fire. "And these gathered about us are your deeds, Your Grace. Your good deeds and your bad deeds. Your good deeds hope to carry you up with them to heaven, and the others—the others wish to follow you to hell and gnaw upon your bones."

"And which of them will have me in the end?"

"I shall not say. I come to keep them all in check until the time is right." Death, who intended to leer down and breathe raggedly into The Emperor's pained face, looked up instead. "What is that?" he growled, his gaze fixing upon the open window while around him the curious little beings who were The Emperor's deeds began to scurry about upon the bedclothes.

"Wh-what is what?" asked Amber fearfully.

"That," whispered Death, rising from off The Emperor's chest and floating like a cloud toward the window. "That."

Amber strove to hear.

"That," whispered Death again. "It calls to me and I cannot resist its call." And of a sudden Death was sailing out the window into the rising sun, the curious little creatures that were The Emperor's good deeds and bad deeds rushing to catch hold of Death's tattered and trailing winding sheet and disappearing out the window with him. And from the gardens, Amber heard the sweet, rich song of the real nightingale, drawing Death away into the early dawn, away into morning and sunrise, away from him.

The weight gone from his chest, the duke began to breathe a good deal easier. He lay still for a moment longer, and then pushed aside the bedclothes and struggled to stand. With cautious steps he made his way to the window and stared out. Death was nowhere to be seen. Stare as he might, Amber saw only the rising sun and the flowers and blue sky. Just as he turned from the window, relieved, the drab little nightingale fluttered in to him and perched upon his shoulder.

"Are you all right?" she asked worriedly. "I did not know that Death had crept so very near, until I heard your Molly speaking to her father before she left him this morning."

"I cannot thank you enough," murmured the duke, offering her his finger to step upon and carrying her back to his bed. "You have saved my life. And after I—after I—" The Emperor did not finish his sentence. A great lump of thankfulness and relief and shame, too, rose up into his throat, and tears rose into his eyes and whispered down his cheeks.

"How did Death come so close?" asked the nightingale.

"I do not know. I thought I loved and was loved in return, and when I found I had deluded myself—"

"You did not believe me when I told you," the nightingale interrupted, fluttering her feathers as one of the Emperor's tears dropped down upon her head. "I will tell you again, then, and this time you must believe. You do love and are loved in return. You have always loved and been loved. And you will always love and be loved—by me—by me—" sang the bird, hopping from his finger to the top of the bejeweled nightingale and from there to the floor.

Just as The Emperor bent to reach for the bird, a brilliant light whizzed in through the window and hummed past his ear. "The Emperor's tears are priceless," a tiny voice declared. And then the light spun in a circle above the nightingale, and the sun came to glow and sparkle at Amber's feet. "By me—by me—" he heard the nightingale continue to sing as the light looped about the room and then whizzed back out into the gardens.

Amber reached down to lift the nightingale up into his hands, fearful that something dreadful had happened to her. But what he caught in his hands were not feathers, but soft, dainty hands, and what he lifted from the floor was not a nightingale, but the loveliest—and nakedest—woman he had ever seen.

His heart beat so rapidly and his head spun so dizzily that he thought he would expire upon the spot. But he pulled himself together and seized his robe from the foot of the bed and wrapped it around her. Her brown hair glittered with gold and her brown eyes glowed with happiness. The freckles upon her nose seemed to dance with glee and her lips smiled the most complacent smile. The Emperor hugged her to him and kissed her chin and her cheek and her nose and her brow and at the last those welcoming lips. "Fiona," he cried, filled with a love that even poets could not write. "Fiona, my darling!"

Nearly smothered in his embrace, she laughed, and the laugh was the sound of the nightingale's finest song.

"But where did you—how did you—why did you—"

"Hush, Julius," Fiona murmured, kissing him once more. "Say only that you love me as you have always done."

"I love you, Fiona, as I have always done. Yes, I have always done!" he cried excitedly. "It is true! I have always loved you!"

"Say that you always will," she urged him, rubbing her cheek tenderly against his and nibbling at his ear.

"I always will love you. Always."

"And promise that when we are married—for your mama will not hold out against the daughter of a gamekeeper as she ought, not once she sees the love that glows in your eyes—promise that you will never allow our children to go poking around those dreadful faeries. They make one's wishes come true without the least thought for what may follow after. I thought I should remain a nightingale forever. Thank goodness one of them was bright enough to think to change me back at last." And then she laughed the fullest, finest, most wonderful laugh.

Well, astonishment veritably flew through Bright that morning. The dowager duchess and Lord Monmouth, the Duke and Duchess of Haarinshire, Lady Elizabeth and Margaret and all the wedding guests, who had been expecting to hear the sad news of The Emperor's death and who had all been overcome with grief just to think of it, were astounded to see His Grace come strolling into the breakfast room with a remarkably beautiful lady upon his arm and a remarkably satisfied smile upon his face. He introduced her as Miss Nightingale and declared that his marriage to

Lady Elizabeth having come acropper—which they had all surmised by then, of course, because gossip did get around—he would be married in the gardens regardless. He would marry Miss Nightingale. And he did exactly that, and the two of them lived happily ever after. Only his mama and Nathan and Margaret were ever told the true tale of what had happened to Fiona Lure, and how Julius had found her again. And each one of them rejoiced in the tale.

Neverby, however, surmised his own surmises, as well he might, having been pressed into service to find clothing for the young lady before His Grace could lead her down the staircase that fateful morning. Each time Neverby looked upon his new mistress he knew her for the real nightingale and loved her for saving his master's life, and he never said "Rotworms!" again. Not even when he was most upset. He smiled and said "Nightingales!" and that was just as well.

# LOOK FOR THESE REGENCY ROMANCES

SCANDAL'S DAUGHTER          (0-8217-5273-1, $4.50)
by Carola Dunn

A DANGEROUS AFFAIR          (0-8217-5294-4, $4.50)
by Mona Gedney

A SUMMER COURTSHIP          (0-8217-5358-4, $4.50)
by Valerie King

TIME'S TAPESTRY             (0-8217-5381-9, $4.99)
by Joan Overfield

LADY STEPHANIE              (0-8217-5341-X, $4.50)
by Jeanne Savery

*Available wherever paperbacks are sold, or order direct from the Publisher. Send cover price plus 50¢ per copy for mailing and handling to Kensington Publishing Corp., Consumer Orders, or call (toll free) 888-345-BOOK, to place your order using Mastercard or Visa. Residents of New York and Tennessee must include sales tax. DO NOT SEND CASH.*